# The Island of the Immortals

**Fairy tales, Folk tales, Legends & Mythology, Volume 10**

Patrick William Lee

Published by Starlit Tales Publishing, 2024.

THE ISLAND OF THE IMMORTALS

**First edition. September 4, 2024.**



ISBN: 979-8227031297

Written by Patrick William Lee.

# Table of Contents

To the dreamers, the seekers, and those brave enough to chase the unknown.

This book is for the adventurers who dare to question what lies beyond the horizon and who understand that the true treasure is not in what we find, but in how we live the journey.

And to those who have stood by me, believed in me, and helped me tell this tale—your support is my true immortality.

With endless gratitude,

P.W.L.

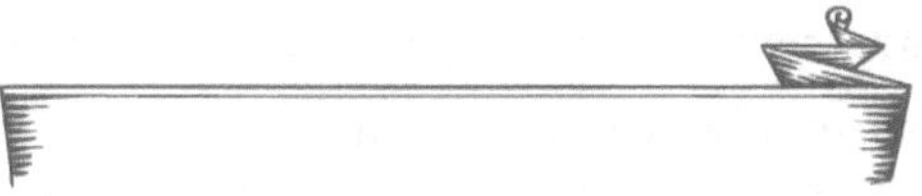

# Chapter 1: The Forgotten Prophecy

In the heart of the ancient kingdom of Elandor, nestled deep within the towering peaks of the Mount Xaren, there existed a legend so old and so powerful that it had become nothing more than whispers on the lips of the elders, dismissed by the young as mere folklore. The legend spoke of a mystical island hidden beyond the known seas, shrouded in mist and mystery. On this island, it was said, lived the Immortals—beings who had transcended death itself. Mortals who set foot on this fabled land could obtain eternal life, but at a cost known only to those who had dared seek it. Many believed the island to be a myth, a story concocted to instill awe and wonder in the hearts of the people.

But for Lyra, the legend had never been just a story. Raised in the shadow of the great Xaren mountains, she had grown up listening to the tales of the island told by her grandmother, a woman whose eyes still gleamed with the light of distant knowledge, even in her old age. Lyra would sit by the hearth as the flames danced, painting flickering shadows on the stone walls, and listen with rapt attention as her grandmother spoke of ships that had set sail to find the Island of the Immortals and the brave souls who never returned. The fire's crackle would merge with her soft, wise voice, weaving a world of adventure and danger that captivated the young Lyra's imagination.

"It's not just a story, you know," her grandmother had said one night, her voice low and serious. Lyra had been no older than ten at the time, but the words had sunk into her like a seed into fertile soil. "The island exists, and the prophecy foretells of a time when one would find it again. But beware, child, for the island is not for the faint of heart. Many seek immortality, but few understand its true price."

Now, years later, Lyra was no longer a child. She had grown into a determined young woman with the spirit of an adventurer. The people of Elandor knew her as a brave soul, always wandering through the forests and mountains, charting territories most would avoid, driven by an insatiable curiosity that seemed almost otherworldly. She had no family left—her grandmother had passed years ago, and her parents had succumbed to a mysterious illness when she was still a baby. Lyra had been raised by the village, but the mountains and the wilds had been her true guardians. She had learned survival, not from books or tutors, but from the land itself.

It was during one of her many treks into the mountains that her life would change forever.

The sun was setting, casting a golden glow over the jagged peaks of Mount Xaren. Lyra was high in the mountains, far from the village, searching for a rare herb that only bloomed at twilight. The crisp mountain air filled her lungs as she scaled a steep incline, her leather boots slipping slightly on the loose rocks. The familiar thrill of exploration surged through her as she climbed higher, her gaze scanning the horizon for any sign of the herb.

As she reached the summit, she paused to catch her breath, her eyes drifting over the expansive view of the valley below. From this height, the world looked peaceful, the village a tiny speck in the distance, the river a silver ribbon winding through the landscape. But Lyra's attention was soon drawn to something unusual—a dark opening in the side of the mountain, half-hidden by overgrown vines and rocks. It wasn't marked on any map she had ever seen, and that piqued her curiosity.

With her heart pounding in her chest, Lyra approached the entrance cautiously. It appeared to be an ancient cave, its stone walls worn smooth by time. There were markings on the entrance, strange symbols etched into the rock that she didn't recognize. They seemed old, far older than the village itself, and they sent a shiver down her spine.

Taking a deep breath, she stepped inside.

The cave was dark, the air cool and damp. Lyra pulled a torch from her pack and lit it, the flame flickering to life and casting a warm glow on the stone walls. As she moved deeper into the cave, the passage widened, revealing a large chamber. In the center of the room stood a stone pedestal, and on it lay a weathered scroll, its edges frayed with age.

Lyra's heart raced as she approached the pedestal. The scroll looked ancient, its surface covered in the same strange symbols she had seen outside. She reached out hesitantly, her fingers brushing the rough parchment. As soon as she touched it, a low rumble echoed through the cave, and the symbols on the scroll began to glow faintly.

Startled, she pulled her hand back, but the glowing didn't stop. The symbols seemed to pulse with energy, and as Lyra watched in awe, they began to shift and change, rearranging themselves into a language she could understand. It was then that she realized what she was looking at—it was the prophecy her grandmother had spoken of, the prophecy of the Island of the Immortals.

With trembling hands, Lyra unrolled the scroll. The writing was clear now, the ancient script transformed into words she could read.

_"When the stars align and the sea grows calm, the path to the Island of the Immortals will reveal itself. Only one with a heart pure of purpose shall find the way. Beware, for the journey is fraught with peril, and the cost of immortality is not one to be taken lightly."_

Lyra's breath caught in her throat. This was it—the prophecy, the key to finding the island. She had always believed in its existence, but to see it written before her, to know that the path could be found, filled her with both excitement and dread.

As she continued to read, the prophecy detailed the steps needed to reach the island. It spoke of a map, hidden within the kingdom, that would guide the way. The map was said to be concealed in a place where the sun never sets, a riddle that intrigued Lyra. But it was the final line of the prophecy that chilled her the most.

_"To gain eternal life is to forsake what once was. To leave the island is to leave behind the gift."_

Lyra stood in silence, the weight of the words pressing down on her. The legend of the island had always fascinated her, but now that she was faced with the reality of its existence, she found herself questioning whether the quest was one worth pursuing. What was the true cost of immortality? And was it a price she was willing to pay?

Lyra returned to the village under the cover of night, her mind racing with the discovery she had made. The prophecy was real, and the island was within reach—but she knew she couldn't do this alone. She needed help, and there was only one person she trusted enough to share this secret with.

Talon.

Talon had been her closest friend for as long as she could remember. They had grown up together, exploring the mountains and forests, always seeking adventure. While Lyra was known for her boundless curiosity, Talon was known for his wisdom and caution. He was the grounding force to her restless spirit, and she knew that if anyone could help her make sense of the prophecy, it was him.

As she reached the edge of the village, she made her way to Talon's workshop. He was a skilled blacksmith, his hands capable of forging weapons and tools as strong as the mountain itself. The glow of the forge cast long shadows across the stone walls as Lyra approached, the familiar clang of metal on metal echoing through the night.

"Talon!" she called, stepping inside.

Talon looked up from his work, his dark eyes narrowing in concern as he saw the urgency in her expression. He set down his hammer and wiped his hands on a cloth before crossing the room to meet her.

"Lyra, what's wrong?" he asked, his voice calm but alert.

She hesitated for a moment, unsure of how to begin. How could she explain what she had found, the magnitude of it?

"I found something in the mountains," she said finally. "Something... incredible."

Talon raised an eyebrow, his curiosity piqued. "What did you find?"

Lyra took a deep breath and told him everything. She described the cave, the strange symbols, the glowing scroll, and the prophecy that had revealed itself to her. As she spoke, Talon listened intently, his expression growing more serious with each word.

When she finished, there was a long silence.

"The Island of the Immortals," Talon said softly, almost to himself. "I've heard the stories, but I never thought..."

"I know," Lyra interrupted. "I didn't think it was real either. But it is. And there's a map—a map that will lead us to the island. I have to find it, Talon. I have to know the truth."

Talon stared at her for a moment, his brow furrowed in thought. Finally, he sighed and ran a hand through his dark hair.

"You know what this means, don't you?" he said. "If the prophecy is real, then so are the dangers. This isn't just some story, Lyra. People have died searching for that island."

"I know," she said quietly. "But I have to try. I've spent my whole life searching for something—something more. And now I've found it. I can't walk away from this."

Talon's gaze softened, and he placed a hand on her shoulder. "I understand. But if you're going to do this, you're not doing it alone. I'll help you."

Lyra smiled, relief flooding through her. She had expected Talon to be cautious, maybe even try to talk her out of it, but she should have known better. Talon had always stood by her side, no matter how dangerous the adventure.

"Thank you," she said, her voice filled with gratitude.

He nodded, a small smile playing on his lips. "We'll find this map. And if the island exists, we'll find that too."

The next morning, Lyra and Talon set out on their quest to uncover the hidden map. The prophecy had been vague, but the line "a place where the sun never sets" lingered in Lyra's mind. She spent hours poring over old texts and consulting the village's wisest elders, trying to decipher the riddle.

It wasn't until they spoke with the village's librarian, an old woman named Halia, that they received their first real clue.

Halia was as ancient as the books she cared for, her frail body bent with age, but her mind was sharp as ever. When Lyra told her about the prophecy, Halia's eyes had sparkled with interest.

"A place where the sun never sets..." Halia mused, tapping her chin thoughtfully. "There is only one place in Elandor that fits that description."

"Where?" Lyra asked eagerly.

"The Great Hall of Records," Halia said, her voice low and mysterious. "It is said that the Hall is bathed in the light of a magical flame that never goes out, a flame that burns as bright as the sun, even in the darkest night."

Lyra exchanged a glance with Talon, excitement bubbling in her chest.

"The Hall of Records," Talon said slowly. "Of course. It's the oldest structure in Elandor. If the map is hidden anywhere, it would be there."

Lyra nodded in agreement. The Hall of Records was a massive stone building located at the heart of the kingdom. It housed ancient texts and artifacts from centuries past, many of which were said to contain powerful magic. It made sense that the map would be hidden there.

Without wasting any time, Lyra and Talon made their way to the Hall of Records. The towering stone structure loomed over them as they approached, its arched doors and intricate carvings giving it an air of mystery and grandeur.

Inside, the Hall was dimly lit, with rows upon rows of dusty shelves filled with books and scrolls. At the center of the room stood a large brazier, and in it burned a bright, golden flame—the flame that Halia had spoken of. It cast long shadows on the walls, giving the Hall an ethereal glow.

"This is it," Lyra whispered as she stared at the flame. "This is where the map is hidden."

Talon nodded, his gaze scanning the room. "The question is, where?"

They spent hours searching the Hall, combing through old texts and examining every inch of the stone walls for hidden compartments or clues. But as the day wore on, they found nothing.

Lyra was beginning to feel frustrated when Talon called her over to one of the shelves near the brazier.

"Look at this," he said, pointing to a small, unassuming book tucked between two larger volumes.

Lyra pulled the book from the shelf and opened it. Inside, the pages were blank—except for one, where a single sentence was written in the same strange symbols she had seen in the cave.

As she stared at the symbols, they began to shift and change, just as they had with the prophecy, transforming into words she could understand.

_"The map lies where the eternal flame meets the light of the stars."_

Lyra looked up at Talon, her heart racing. "The eternal flame," she repeated. "It's the brazier. The map is hidden near the brazier."

They hurried over to the brazier, examining it closely. At first glance, it appeared to be nothing more than a large metal basin filled with fire. But as Lyra crouched down to inspect the base, she noticed something—a faint outline of a compartment hidden beneath the stone floor.

"This is it," she said, her voice barely a whisper.

Together, she and Talon pried open the hidden compartment. Inside, lying on a bed of silk, was an old, tattered scroll—the map.

Lyra's hands trembled as she reached for it, unrolling the fragile parchment with care. The map was unlike any she had ever seen. It was not a map of the known world, but of a realm beyond—an unknown sea, with a single island marked in the center. The Island of the Immortals.

"We found it," Talon breathed.

Lyra stared at the map, her heart pounding in her chest. The prophecy had been true. The island was real, and now she held the key to finding it.

But as she looked at the map, a sense of unease settled over her. The journey ahead would not be easy. The prophecy had warned of the dangers, and Lyra knew that the path to the Island of the Immortals would be fraught with peril.

Yet despite the fear that gnawed at the edges of her mind, she felt a sense of purpose unlike anything she had ever known. This was her destiny—the adventure she had been waiting for her entire life.

And she would not turn back now.

As Lyra and Talon left the Hall of Records, the ancient map clutched tightly in her hands, the first stars began to appear in the night sky. The prophecy had been fulfilled, the quest set in motion.

The Island of the Immortals awaited.

END OF CHAPTER 1.

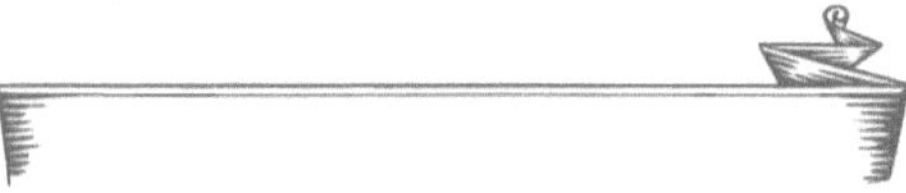

# Chapter 2: The Call to Adventure

Lyra had barely slept since the night she and Talon discovered the map to the Island of the Immortals. The excitement of the discovery pulsed through her veins, as potent as the glowing symbols she had witnessed in the cave. She felt as though she had stumbled upon a secret that had been waiting for her all her life, hidden in the folds of time, just beyond the reach of ordinary mortals. And now that the secret had revealed itself, she couldn't ignore its call.

But as the first rays of dawn began to peek over the jagged peaks of Mount Xaren, casting long shadows over the village, doubt crept into her mind. The weight of the prophecy still hung heavy on her thoughts, and she knew she couldn't embark on such a perilous journey without seeking guidance. The Island of the Immortals was no ordinary destination. Legends had long warned of the dangers that awaited those who sought it out, and though she had the map, Lyra knew there were more mysteries she needed to unravel before she set sail.

So, she did what she knew she must: she would consult the elders.

The elders of Elandor were not just leaders of the village; they were keepers of its history, guardians of its myths and stories. Each elder held a piece of knowledge passed down through generations, knowledge that had shaped the very foundation of their world. If anyone could help her understand the gravity of her discovery—and the dangers it posed—it was them.

The elder council resided in the Hall of Wisdom, an ancient building on the edge of the village, its stone walls covered in moss and vines, a testament to its age. The great wooden doors of the hall loomed before her as Lyra approached, her heart beating fast in her chest. She had visited the Hall of Wisdom many times as a child, accompanying her grandmother, who had often been summoned to share her knowledge of the old ways. But this time felt different. This time, she was seeking answers for herself.

Talon walked beside her, silent but ever watchful, his steady presence a source of comfort. He had been just as shaken by the discovery of the map as she had, but he shared her belief that this was more than just a tale—it was real, and it was dangerous.

"Are you sure about this?" Talon asked quietly as they reached the doors. His voice was calm, but Lyra could sense the tension beneath it. "Once you bring the elders into this, there's no turning back. They'll expect answers."

"I know," Lyra said, her hand resting on the worn wood of the door. "But I can't ignore it, Talon. I have to know what they think. I have to understand what I'm getting myself into."

Talon nodded, his dark eyes filled with understanding. "Then let's do this."

With a deep breath, Lyra pushed open the heavy doors, the groaning of the wood echoing in the quiet morning air. Inside, the Hall of Wisdom was dimly lit by candles and the morning sun filtering through small windows high in the walls. The smell of incense hung in the air, mingling with the faint scent of old books and parchment.

The elders were seated in a semicircle at the far end of the hall, their faces partially obscured by the shadows. There were five of them, each one older than the last, their expressions unreadable as Lyra and Talon approached. The central figure, Elder Teren, was the oldest and most respected of the council. His long white beard reached his chest, and his sharp eyes seemed to see right through Lyra as she stood before him.

"Lyra," Elder Teren said, his voice slow and deliberate. "You have come seeking counsel, but I can see in your eyes that you carry a heavy burden. What brings you before us today?"

Lyra swallowed the lump in her throat and stepped forward, her gaze flicking to each of the elders in turn before returning to Teren. "Elders, I have come because I have made a discovery—one that could change everything."

The room fell silent, and the weight of their attention pressed down on her like a physical force. She hesitated for a moment, unsure of how to begin, but then the words tumbled out, and she told them everything. The cave, the prophecy, the glowing symbols, and finally, the map. As she spoke, the expressions of the elders remained impassive, but their eyes betrayed the gravity of her revelation.

When she finished, there was a long pause. Elder Teren stroked his beard thoughtfully, his gaze fixed on Lyra, while the other elders exchanged quiet glances.

Finally, it was Elder Meron, the youngest of the council, who spoke. "The Island of the Immortals," she said, her voice filled with a quiet reverence. "It has been centuries since anyone dared to speak of it openly. The last person to seek it out never returned. What you have found is not just a map, Lyra—it is a key to something far more dangerous than you realize."

Lyra felt a chill run down her spine at Meron's words. "I know it's dangerous," she said, her voice steady. "But I believe this is my path. The prophecy spoke of someone who would find the way, and now that I have the map, I can't turn back. I need to understand what lies ahead."

Elder Teren nodded slowly, his eyes narrowing in thought. "The Island of the Immortals is not a place for mortals, Lyra. It is a place where the line between life and death is blurred, where the cost of immortality is greater than most can bear. Many have sought it, but few have returned. Those who did were... changed."

Lyra's stomach tightened at the ominous warning. "Changed how?"

Teren leaned forward slightly, his voice lowering to a near whisper. "They were no longer themselves. Their minds were... fractured, as though the very act of seeking immortality had broken something within them. They spoke of visions, of beings that could not be seen by mortal eyes. And they warned of the price—of a cost so great that no man or woman could truly understand it."

Lyra's heart raced, but she forced herself to remain calm. "Then why does the prophecy exist? Why speak of the island at all if no one is meant to find it?"

"The prophecy," Teren said, his gaze piercing, "was never meant to be a guide. It was meant as a warning. The path to the island may reveal itself, but it is not a path that should be taken lightly. The island is a place of power, and power has always been dangerous."

Lyra bit her lip, her mind swirling with questions. She had always known the journey would be dangerous, but now that the elders had confirmed the legends, the weight of what she was about to undertake felt even heavier.

Still, despite their warnings, she felt a pull—a deep, instinctive urge that she couldn't ignore. It was as if the island itself was calling to her, beckoning her forward, even as the elders cautioned her to stay away.

"I understand the dangers," she said finally, her voice steady. "But this is my choice. I have always felt that there was something more out there, something I was meant to find. And now that I've found the map, I know this is what I must do."

The elders exchanged glances once more, and for a moment, Lyra feared they would forbid her from pursuing the journey. But then Teren spoke, his voice filled with a quiet resignation.

"You are brave, Lyra," he said. "But bravery alone will not see you through this journey. You must be prepared for the trials ahead, and you must understand that the choice you make will not only affect you, but all those who journey with you. The Island of the Immortals is a place where lives are changed—forever."

Lyra nodded, her resolve firm. "I will gather those who are willing to take the risk with me. I will not force anyone to follow me, but I cannot do this alone."

Teren's gaze softened slightly, and he gave her a small, approving nod. "Very well. You have our blessing, but know this: the road ahead is long, and it is filled with shadows. Do not let the promise of immortality blind you to the dangers that lie in wait."

"I won't," Lyra promised, her heart pounding in her chest.

As she and Talon left the Hall of Wisdom, the gravity of her decision settled heavily on her shoulders. The elders had given her their blessing, but they had also given her something far more valuable—knowledge of the true dangers she would face. Now, it was up to her to gather those who would join her on the quest.

The village of Elandor was small, but it was filled with people of all kinds—farmers, blacksmiths, hunters, and scholars. Lyra knew that she would need a diverse group of companions if she was going to survive the journey to the Island of the Immortals. She needed people with different skills, people who could help her navigate the unknown.

The first person she approached was Galen, the village's most skilled hunter. He was a tall, broad-shouldered man with a sharp wit and even sharper reflexes.

Lyra had known Galen for years, and she knew he was no stranger to danger. He had survived more than one encounter with wild beasts, and his knowledge of tracking and survival would be invaluable on the journey ahead.

She found him in the village square, trading pelts for supplies with one of the merchants. When she approached, Galen greeted her with a grin, his dark eyes glinting with mischief.

"Lyra!" he said, clapping her on the shoulder. "What brings you to the square? Looking for trouble, as usual?"

Lyra smiled, but there was no humor in her eyes. "Actually, I am looking for trouble—though not the kind you're thinking of."

Galen raised an eyebrow, his grin fading slightly. "What do you mean?"

Lyra took a deep breath and told him everything—about the prophecy, the map, and the journey to the Island of the Immortals. As she spoke, Galen's expression grew more serious, and by the time she finished, he was frowning.

"The Island of the Immortals?" he said, crossing his arms over his chest. "I've heard the stories, Lyra. No one who goes there ever comes back the same. If they come back at all."

"I know," Lyra said. "But I have to do this, Galen. I need to understand what's out there. And I can't do it alone."

Galen stared at her for a long moment, his brow furrowed in thought. Finally, he sighed and uncrossed his arms. "You're crazy, you know that?"

"Probably," Lyra said with a shrug. "But I need your help."

Galen chuckled, shaking his head. "Well, I've never been one to back down from a challenge. If you're going to do this, you'll need someone who knows how to survive out there. And I suppose that's me."

Lyra smiled, relief flooding through her. "Thank you, Galen."

"Don't thank me yet," he said, his grin returning. "We haven't even started."

The next person Lyra sought out was Kael, a skilled healer who had once served in the king's army before retiring to Elandor to live a quieter life. Kael was known throughout the village for his knowledge of herbs and medicine, and his ability to mend wounds that others deemed untreatable. Lyra knew that if she and her companions were going to survive the dangers of the journey, they would need someone with Kael's skills.

She found him tending to his herb garden outside his small cottage on the outskirts of the village. He was an older man, his hair streaked with gray, but his eyes were sharp and intelligent.

"Kael," Lyra called as she approached. "I need your help."

Kael looked up from his work, his brow furrowing slightly. "What's wrong, Lyra? You don't usually seek me out unless someone's hurt."

"It's not that," Lyra said, shaking her head. "I'm going on a journey—a dangerous one. And I need someone with your knowledge of healing."

Kael straightened, wiping his hands on a cloth. "A dangerous journey, you say? What kind of danger are we talking about?"

Lyra hesitated for a moment, then told him about the Island of the Immortals and the prophecy. She explained the risks, the dangers, and the uncertainty of what lay ahead. Kael listened quietly, his expression growing more serious with each passing moment.

When she finished, Kael was silent for a long time, his eyes distant as he considered her words. Finally, he sighed and looked at her with a mixture of concern and admiration.

"You're a brave girl, Lyra," he said softly. "But bravery alone won't protect you from the dangers you'll face. If you're going to do this, you'll need more than just my healing skills. You'll need to be prepared for the worst."

"I know," Lyra said. "That's why I'm asking you to come with me."

Kael stared at her for a long moment, then nodded slowly. "Very well. I'll come. But know this, Lyra—once we start this journey, there may be no turning back."

"I understand," Lyra said. "And I'm ready."

WITH TALON, GALEN, and Kael by her side, Lyra felt more confident about the journey ahead. But there was one more person she needed to recruit—someone with knowledge of the seas. The map had shown that the Island of the Immortals was far beyond the known lands, across an uncharted sea. If they were going to make it there, they needed a skilled sailor.

And there was only one person in Elandor who fit that description.

Sienna.

Sienna was a former pirate, or so the rumors said. She had arrived in Elandor years ago, her past shrouded in mystery. What Lyra knew for certain was that Sienna was one of the best sailors she had ever met. She was fearless, cunning, and had a reputation for being able to navigate even the most treacherous waters. If anyone could get them to the island, it was Sienna.

Lyra found Sienna in the local tavern, nursing a mug of ale and chatting with the barkeep. When Lyra approached, Sienna raised an eyebrow and smirked.

"Well, well," Sienna said, her voice laced with amusement. "What brings the village's resident adventurer to my table?"

"I need your help," Lyra said, sitting down across from her.

Sienna's smirk widened. "Help with what?"

Lyra didn't hesitate this time. She told Sienna about the map, the prophecy, and the Island of the Immortals. As she spoke, Sienna's expression shifted from amusement to intrigue, and by the time Lyra finished, Sienna was leaning forward, her eyes gleaming with excitement.

"The Island of the Immortals, huh?" Sienna said, leaning back in her chair. "Now that's a journey I can get behind. Dangerous, mysterious, and probably illegal. Count me in."

Lyra couldn't help but smile. "Thank you, Sienna."

"Don't thank me yet, sweetheart," Sienna said with a wink. "This isn't going to be easy. But if you're serious about this, then let's make it happen."

With her companions gathered, Lyra stood at the edge of the village, gazing out at the horizon. The journey to the Island of the Immortals was about to begin, and though the path ahead was uncertain, she felt a sense of purpose that filled her with both excitement and trepidation.

The call to adventure had come.

And she was ready to answer.

END OF CHAPTER 2.

# Chapter 3: The Storm of Trials

The sea stretched out endlessly before them, its sapphire waters glittering beneath the morning sun. Lyra stood at the helm of the ship, her hand resting lightly on the worn wooden wheel, her eyes scanning the horizon. The wind tugged at her dark hair, and the smell of salt filled the air, mingling with the distant cries of gulls. For a moment, the world felt peaceful. The rolling waves and the steady rhythm of the ship cutting through the water offered a brief illusion of tranquility, but deep within, Lyra knew better.

Their journey had only just begun, and the calm before the storm was nothing more than a fleeting respite.

Beside her, Sienna stood with an experienced eye on the sails, her tanned hands adjusting the ropes with the ease of someone who had spent most of her life on the water. Every movement she made was deliberate, confident. She was in her element, and despite her roguish demeanor, Lyra was grateful to have her at the helm. Sienna had navigated treacherous seas before, and she was unafraid of what lay ahead.

Behind them, Galen leaned against the railing, his sharp eyes scanning the distant horizon for signs of trouble, while Kael sat cross-legged near the mast, sharpening a small dagger with calm precision. Talon was below deck, organizing the supplies they had brought for the journey. The ship, though sturdy, was old, a relic of a time when Elandor's navy had been strong. It had taken some convincing to borrow it from the village's harbor master, but with Sienna's skill and charm, they had managed to secure it for their quest.

The air was thick with anticipation, the silence between them punctuated only by the creak of wood and the soft lapping of waves against the hull. None of them spoke much. The weight of the journey ahead hung heavy over the group, a shadow they could not shake.

Lyra's mind, however, was not on the peaceful scene around her. It was on the map, the prophecy, and the island that seemed both impossibly close and impossibly far. She had memorized every line of the map, every cryptic symbol and warning it held, but none of that could prepare her for the uncertainty of what lay ahead. The Island of the Immortals was a place shrouded in legend, a realm where no mortal had ventured and returned unchanged. And now, as they sailed toward that fabled island, she couldn't help but wonder if they would survive long enough to see it.

A chill ran down her spine, and she pulled her cloak tighter around her shoulders, despite the warmth of the sun.

Sienna, noticing her discomfort, shot her a sideways glance. "Feeling uneasy, Lyra?"

Lyra nodded, forcing a smile. "Just thinking. About what's to come."

Sienna gave a low chuckle, her eyes fixed on the horizon. "That's the thing about the sea. It forces you to think about what you can't control. You never know what's coming—could be smooth sailing for days, or a storm out of nowhere. But you have to be ready for both."

The words settled uneasily in Lyra's mind. She had felt it too, an ominous undercurrent in the air. The sea was too calm, the sky too clear. It was the kind of stillness that often preceded chaos. And the longer they sailed, the stronger that feeling became.

Galen joined them at the helm, his face grim. "We're heading into uncharted waters now," he said, his voice low. "The village elders spoke of strange occurrences in this part of the sea—disappearances, sudden storms, ships lost without a trace."

Lyra nodded. She had heard the same stories, passed down from sailor to sailor, each tale more terrifying than the last. Ships that vanished into thin air, swallowed by the sea, never to be seen again. It was why so few dared to venture into these waters.

But they had no choice. The map pointed them in this direction, and they had to follow it, no matter what.

Sienna tightened her grip on the wheel, her expression unreadable. "If a storm's coming, we'll face it. I've seen worse."

As if the sea had heard her words, the sky began to darken. Clouds gathered on the horizon, their edges tinged with an unnatural shade of green. The wind picked up, sharp and biting, and the gentle lapping of the waves turned into a deep, foreboding roar. The calm was broken, and the first signs of the storm began to take shape.

Lyra's heart raced as she watched the storm approach, her pulse quickening with every gust of wind. "We should lower the sails," she called out over the rising wind. "We're heading straight into it."

But Sienna shook her head, her jaw clenched. "We can't outrun it, Lyra. We have to ride it out. Lowering the sails now will leave us at the mercy of the waves."

Before Lyra could respond, a deafening crack split the air, and a bolt of lightning lit up the sky, illuminating the rapidly growing storm. The waves swelled, rising higher and higher, and the ship began to pitch and roll beneath them. The wind howled, ripping through the sails, and the once-calm sea became a swirling maelstrom of chaos.

"Hold on!" Sienna shouted as the ship lurched violently to one side, nearly throwing them off their feet.

Lyra grabbed onto the railing, her knuckles white as she struggled to maintain her balance. The storm had arrived with a fury unlike anything she had ever experienced. The sky was black, the rain coming down in sheets so thick that it was nearly impossible to see more than a few feet ahead. The wind screamed, tearing at the ship, and the waves crashed against the hull with a force that shook the entire vessel.

"Sienna, we need to steer clear of the waves!" Galen shouted, his voice barely audible over the storm. "We'll be smashed to pieces if we don't!"

Sienna's face was set in grim determination as she fought to keep the ship steady. "I know!" she shouted back. "But this storm isn't natural. Something's not right."

Lyra could feel it too. The storm wasn't just a force of nature—it felt deliberate, as though it had been summoned by some unseen hand. The prophecy had warned of trials, of tests that would challenge them before they could reach the Island of the Immortals. Was this one of them? A trial designed to test their resolve, to see if they were worthy of continuing the journey?

As the ship lurched again, Lyra lost her grip on the railing and was thrown to the deck. Pain shot through her side as she hit the hard wood, but she pushed herself up, her heart pounding. They couldn't let the storm defeat them. They had come too far.

"Talon!" she shouted, her voice barely carrying over the wind. "Kael! We need to secure the cargo!"

Talon appeared at the entrance to the lower deck, his face pale but determined. He nodded and disappeared below, followed closely by Kael. The supplies they had brought for the journey were essential, and if the storm swept them overboard, they would be stranded with nothing.

Lyra scrambled to her feet, clutching the railing as the ship rocked violently beneath her. Water sloshed over the deck, soaking her to the bone, and the wind tore at her cloak, threatening to rip it from her shoulders. The sky was a blur of darkness and lightning, and the sound of the storm was deafening.

But through the chaos, Lyra felt something else—something deeper, more ancient than the storm itself. It was as if the sea, the wind, and the sky were alive, testing them, pushing them to their limits. The prophecy had spoken of trials, and this was the first. The storm was not just a storm—it was a test of their strength, their resolve, and their unity as a group.

And they would have to face it together.

Lyra forced her way toward the helm, where Sienna was still fighting to keep the ship on course. "We need to work together!" Lyra shouted over the wind. "We can't survive this alone!"

Sienna glanced at her, her eyes hard but filled with understanding. She nodded once, then barked out orders to the rest of the crew.

"Galen, get the ropes and secure the mast! Lyra, help me with the wheel!"

Galen moved quickly, his powerful arms pulling the ropes tight as he secured the mast, while Lyra grabbed hold of the wheel beside Sienna, using all her strength to help steer the ship through the towering waves. Together, they fought against the storm, their combined efforts keeping the ship from capsizing.

The storm raged on, relentless in its fury. The waves grew higher, crashing over the deck and threatening to sweep them all into the sea. Lightning split the sky, followed by deafening claps of thunder that shook the ship to its core. The sails flapped wildly in the wind, torn and tattered, but still they held.

Lyra's muscles burned with the effort of holding the wheel steady, and her heart raced with fear and adrenaline. But despite the terror of the storm, she felt a strange sense of unity with her companions. They were all fighting together, relying on each other's strength to survive. Each person played a crucial role, and without that cooperation, they would have been lost.

The storm wasn't just testing their physical endurance—it was testing their bond as a group, forcing them to work together in the face of overwhelming danger.

Minutes turned into hours as they battled the storm, and still it showed no signs of relenting. The sky remained a swirling mass of black clouds and lightning, the wind howling like a living thing. But slowly, steadily, they began to find their rhythm. Galen's skill with the ropes kept the mast secure, while Kael and Talon worked below deck to keep the ship from flooding. Sienna and Lyra, side by side at the helm, steered the ship with precision and determination, guiding it through the worst of the waves.

For the first time since the storm had begun, Lyra felt a flicker of hope.

"We can do this!" she shouted to Sienna, her voice barely audible over the roar of the wind.

Sienna grinned, her eyes gleaming with fierce determination. "Damn right we can!"

But just as the words left her mouth, the storm seemed to intensify. The wind howled even louder, and the waves grew impossibly high, towering over the ship like massive walls of water. Lyra's heart lurched as she saw the largest wave yet rise before them, its dark, churning surface glistening with foam.

"Sienna!" Lyra shouted, panic creeping into her voice. "We need to turn!"

But it was too late. The wave crashed down on them with a force that sent the entire ship tipping sideways. Lyra was thrown from the wheel, her body slamming into the deck as water engulfed the ship. She gasped for air, her lungs burning as the freezing water dragged her toward the edge.

For a terrifying moment, Lyra thought she would be swept overboard. The force of the water was too strong, and she couldn't find anything to grab onto. Her mind raced, and fear gripped her heart like a vice. Was this how it would end? Drowned in the middle of a storm, before they even reached the island?

But then, through the chaos, she felt a strong hand grab her arm.

"Talon!" she gasped, her eyes wide with relief as she saw him pulling her back from the edge.

"Hold on!" he shouted, his voice barely audible over the roar of the storm.

With Talon's help, Lyra managed to crawl back to the center of the deck, her chest heaving with exertion. The ship was still rocking violently, but they had survived the worst of the wave. Galen and Kael were soaked but still holding their positions, their faces grim with determination.

Lyra looked up at the sky, her heart pounding. The storm was relentless, but she refused to give up. They had made it this far, and they would make it through the storm, no matter what.

Sienna, though battered and exhausted, still stood at the helm, her hands gripping the wheel tightly. "We're not out of this yet!" she shouted, her voice hoarse but filled with resolve. "But we're getting closer! Hold on!"

The storm raged on, but as the hours passed, Lyra began to notice a change. The waves, though still dangerous, were no longer as towering as they had been before. The wind, though fierce, was beginning to die down. And the rain, once a torrential downpour, was starting to lighten.

Slowly, gradually, the storm began to recede.

By the time the first rays of sunlight broke through the clouds, the sea had returned to a more manageable state. The waves still rocked the ship, but the worst of the storm had passed.

Lyra collapsed onto the deck, her body aching and her muscles trembling with exhaustion. She had never been so tired in her life, but a deep sense of relief washed over her. They had survived.

Talon knelt beside her, his face pale but relieved. "You did it," he said, his voice soft.

Lyra shook her head, a tired smile on her lips. "We did it. Together."

Sienna, drenched but grinning, walked over to them, her eyes sparkling with pride. "Not bad for your first storm, huh?"

Lyra laughed, though the sound was weak. "I'd rather not do that again anytime soon."

Galen and Kael joined them, both looking equally exhausted but relieved. They had all survived the first trial, and though they were battered and bruised, they were still standing.

The storm, though fierce and terrifying, had tested them in ways they hadn't expected. It had forced them to rely on each other, to work together, and to push beyond their limits. And in doing so, it had strengthened their bond as a group.

But Lyra knew this was only the beginning. The storm had been the first trial, but it wouldn't be the last. The Island of the Immortals was still far ahead, and there were more challenges to come.

As the sun rose over the horizon, casting its golden light across the calm sea, Lyra stood and gazed out at the endless expanse of water. The storm had tested their resolve, and they had passed. But the journey was far from over.

The island awaited, and with it, the unknown trials that lay ahead.

End of Chapter 3.

# Chapter 4: The Island of Shadows

The sea was calm as their ship cut through the glassy waters, the storm now a distant memory. For hours, they had sailed in a strange, almost eerie silence. The wind had died down to a faint whisper, barely enough to fill the sails, and the horizon was shrouded in a thick, unnatural fog. It clung to the air like a living thing, swirling in strange patterns, obscuring everything beyond the ship's bow.

Lyra stood at the helm, her eyes fixed on the mist as it curled and shifted, her heart pounding with a mixture of excitement and unease. They were close—she could feel it. The map had led them to this point, to the edge of the unknown. The Island of the Immortals was near, but something about the fog set her on edge.

Beside her, Sienna tightened her grip on the wheel, her usually confident demeanor tinged with a hint of wariness. The sea had been too calm, the air too still. It was as though the ocean itself was holding its breath, waiting for something to happen.

"Are you sure this is the right direction?" Talon asked, his voice low as he joined them at the helm.

Lyra nodded, though uncertainty gnawed at the edges of her resolve. "The map led us here. We're close."

Talon glanced at the fog, his brow furrowing. "But where is 'here'? That fog doesn't look natural."

"It isn't," Sienna muttered under her breath. "I've sailed through a lot of strange waters, but this... this is different."

Galen, who had been leaning against the railing, his sharp eyes scanning the horizon, pushed himself upright and approached them. "Different how?"

Sienna's eyes narrowed as she studied the fog. "It's too thick, too still. Fog like this shouldn't exist on a calm sea. And it feels... wrong."

Lyra could sense it too, a strange heaviness in the air, like the weight of a thousand unseen eyes watching them from within the mist. She glanced down at the map in her hand, tracing the faded lines with her fingers. This was the right place, she was certain of it. But the fog made everything feel uncertain, as if the very world around them was shifting and changing with each passing second.

As the ship sailed deeper into the fog, the temperature began to drop, the warmth of the sun fading behind the thick, swirling clouds. The air grew cold, and a chill settled over the deck, seeping into their bones. The once bright blue of the sea turned a murky gray, the waves almost sluggish as they lapped against the hull.

"We need to keep moving," Lyra said, her voice more confident than she felt. "The map shows that the island is just beyond this fog."

Sienna hesitated for a moment, then nodded, adjusting the sails to guide them further into the mist.

As they ventured deeper, the fog seemed to grow thicker, enveloping the ship in a damp, suffocating shroud. Visibility dropped to mere feet, and the world beyond the bow disappeared entirely. Even the sound of the sea seemed muted, the gentle splashing of the waves against the hull now a distant echo.

"I don't like this," Kael muttered from where he stood near the mast, his arms crossed tightly over his chest. "It feels like we're being watched."

Lyra didn't respond, but she couldn't shake the feeling that he was right. There was something... off about this place, something that made her skin crawl. She tried to push the unease aside, focusing instead on the task at hand. They had come too far to turn back now. The Island of the Immortals was close, and they had to keep going.

For what felt like hours, they sailed in silence, the only sound the occasional creak of the ship's timbers and the soft rustling of the sails. The fog was so thick that it felt as though they were sailing through a dream, a world of shadows and half-formed shapes. Every now and then, Lyra thought she saw movement in the mist—fleeting figures that seemed to dance just beyond the edge of her vision—but when she blinked, they were gone.

"We should have reached the island by now," Galen said, his voice tense. "If the map is accurate, we should be there."

"We are," Sienna said, her voice tight. "I can feel it. We're close."

As if in response to her words, a low, mournful sound echoed through the fog—a deep, resonant hum that sent a shiver down Lyra's spine. It wasn't the sound of the wind or the waves. It was something else, something far older and more haunting.

"What was that?" Talon asked, his hand instinctively going to the hilt of his sword.

Before anyone could answer, the fog began to shift. Slowly, the dense mist parted, revealing the faint outline of land ahead. The ship creaked as it drifted closer, and Lyra's heart leapt in her chest. There, rising out of the fog like a phantom, was the shoreline of a dark, jagged island.

They had found it.

"The Island of the Immortals," Lyra whispered, her breath catching in her throat.

But as they drew nearer, the uneasy feeling in her chest grew stronger. The island was not what she had expected. Instead of lush forests or towering mountains, the landscape before them was barren and desolate. The shore was lined with jagged rocks, and the land beyond was shrouded in shadow, as though the island itself was trapped in perpetual twilight. There were no signs of life, no birds, no animals—only an eerie, oppressive silence that pressed down on them like a weight.

"This doesn't look like any paradise I've ever seen," Galen muttered, his brow furrowed as he stared at the island.

"It's not supposed to be a paradise," Kael said quietly, his voice tinged with something close to fear. "It's a place of power. A place where immortality is earned."

Lyra stepped forward, her eyes fixed on the shore. "We have to go ashore. We've come this far."

Sienna glanced at her, her expression unreadable, then nodded. "Lower the anchor. We'll take the rowboat."

With the anchor dropped, Lyra, Sienna, Talon, Galen, and Kael climbed into the small rowboat and made their way toward the island. The closer they got, the more the oppressive feeling in the air intensified. The fog clung to the shoreline, swirling around them like ghostly fingers as they rowed toward the rocks.

When they finally reached the shore, Lyra was the first to step out onto the jagged rocks. The moment her boots touched the ground, a strange sensation washed over her, as if the very air around her was charged with an ancient, unnatural energy. The island felt... wrong, as though it didn't belong in the world they knew.

The others followed her, their faces tense and alert as they took in their surroundings. The landscape was bleak and unforgiving, the ground beneath their feet cold and hard. A thick layer of mist clung to the ground, swirling around their ankles as they moved further inland.

"This place feels... dead," Talon said, his voice low.

"It's not dead," Kael replied, his gaze distant. "It's waiting."

"Waiting for what?" Galen asked, his hand on the hilt of his sword.

Kael didn't answer.

As they ventured deeper into the island, the fog grew thicker, the shadows longer. The air was cold, and every step they took seemed to echo in the unnatural silence. The trees, if they could be called trees, were twisted and gnarled, their branches reaching out like skeletal fingers. The ground was littered with broken stones and fragments of what looked like ancient ruins, the remnants of a forgotten civilization.

"It's like time doesn't exist here," Sienna muttered, her voice barely above a whisper. "Everything feels... frozen."

Lyra nodded, her heart pounding in her chest. The island was unlike anything she had ever seen. It was as if the very fabric of reality had been twisted and distorted, leaving behind a place that existed outside the normal flow of time and space.

Suddenly, a low, haunting sound echoed through the fog—a soft, mournful wail that sent a chill down Lyra's spine. She froze, her breath catching in her throat as the sound grew louder, more distinct. It was a voice, distant and ethereal, calling out to them from somewhere deep within the mist.

"Did you hear that?" Talon asked, his hand tightening on his sword.

Lyra nodded, her eyes scanning the fog. "It's coming from up ahead."

Without waiting for a response, she moved forward, her footsteps silent on the cold, damp ground. The others followed, their faces tense with anticipation.

As they pressed on, the fog began to thin, revealing a clearing up ahead. In the center of the clearing stood a massive stone archway, its surface covered in strange, ancient symbols that glowed faintly in the dim light. Beyond the archway, the shadows seemed to deepen, as though the very air was thick with darkness.

And standing before the archway were figures—pale, translucent figures that shimmered like ghosts in the fog. They were dressed in tattered, ancient clothing, their faces gaunt and hollow, their eyes empty and soulless.

Lyra's heart raced as she realized what they were. Spirits. The souls of those who had come before them, adventurers who had sought the Island of the Immortals and failed.

The figures turned toward them, their empty eyes fixed on Lyra and her companions. For a long, terrifying moment, no one spoke. The spirits simply stood there, watching, their faces twisted with a mixture of sorrow and warning.

One of the spirits stepped forward, its voice a soft, echoing whisper that seemed to come from all directions at once.

"Turn back," the spirit said, its voice filled with an ancient, weary sadness. "This island is not what you seek."

Lyra swallowed hard, her pulse quickening. "We're looking for the Island of the Immortals. We followed the map—"

"The map led you here," the spirit interrupted, its voice cold and distant. "But this is not the island you seek. This is the Island of Shadows, a place where time stands still and the souls of the lost are trapped."

Lyra's heart sank as the spirit's words washed over her. The Island of Shadows. They had come to the wrong place. But how? The map had been clear, hadn't it?

Sienna stepped forward, her eyes narrowing. "If this isn't the Island of the Immortals, then where is it? We followed the map exactly."

The spirit's hollow eyes fixed on her, and for a moment, it seemed to hesitate. "The island you seek is beyond this place," it said slowly, its voice tinged with something close to pity. "But it is not a place for mortals. Those who seek immortality must first face the trials of this island. Only then will the true path be revealed."

"The trials?" Talon asked, his voice tight with fear. "What kind of trials?"

The spirit didn't answer. Instead, it slowly raised its hand and pointed toward the stone archway. "Beyond this gate lies the realm of shadows. You will face your greatest fears, your deepest regrets. Only those who survive will be granted passage to the Island of the Immortals."

Lyra's stomach churned with a mixture of fear and determination. The prophecy had spoken of trials, but she hadn't expected anything like this. The thought of facing her greatest fears, her deepest regrets... it terrified her.

But they had come too far to turn back now. They had faced the storm, survived the journey across the sea. They couldn't abandon the quest now, not when they were so close.

"We have to do this," Lyra said, her voice steady despite the fear gnawing at her insides. "It's the only way."

Talon and Galen exchanged uneasy glances, but neither of them objected. Sienna's jaw was set in grim determination, and even Kael, who had been the most fearful of the group, nodded in reluctant agreement.

The spirit lowered its hand, its empty eyes filled with sorrow. "Then you must pass through the gate. But know this: many have come before you, and few have returned. The shadows will test you. They will break you if you are not strong enough."

Lyra nodded, her heart pounding in her chest. She stepped forward, her hand reaching out toward the stone archway.

As her fingers brushed the cold stone, the air around her seemed to shift. The fog thickened, the shadows deepened, and the world around them seemed to dissolve into darkness.

The trial had begun.

End of Chapter 4.

# Chapter 5: The Guardian of the Gate

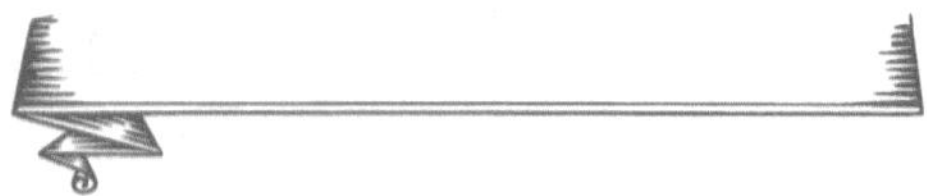

The oppressive fog clung to the ground, swirling in ghostly tendrils as Lyra and her companions stood before the stone archway that loomed like a sentinel at the edge of the Island of Shadows. It was the only path forward, but it was more than just an entrance—it was a test, a threshold that separated the worthy from the unworthy. The spirits had warned them that the trials were far from over, and as Lyra gazed into the dark void beyond the gate, she could feel the weight of that warning pressing down on her shoulders.

Her breath came in shallow, uneven gasps, and she could hear her heart pounding in her ears. They had made it this far, surviving the treacherous journey through the storm and encountering the restless spirits of failed adventurers. But this... this felt different. There was a presence here, something ancient and powerful, watching them from beyond the shadows.

"I don't like this," Galen muttered, his hand resting on the hilt of his sword. His eyes scanned the dense fog that obscured the path ahead, his muscles tense with readiness. "There's something here, something we can't see."

Lyra nodded, her gaze fixed on the archway. "I can feel it too. We're being watched."

Sienna, her brow furrowed, stepped closer to the gate, her sharp eyes narrowing as she studied the ancient stone structure. "This is no ordinary gate," she said quietly, her voice laced with suspicion. "There's magic here—old magic. We won't be able to pass through without facing whatever it is that guards this place."

Talon stepped forward, his sword already drawn, his expression grim. "Then we need to be ready for anything. If this is a trial, we have to pass it."

Kael, who had been uncharacteristically quiet since their encounter with the spirits, finally spoke, his voice low and uncertain. "If the spirits are right, this gate is a test of our worth. We won't be able to fight our way through it like we did the storm."

Lyra knew he was right. The Island of the Immortals wasn't just about physical strength or endurance—it was about something far deeper. Whatever trial awaited them beyond the gate would challenge them in ways they couldn't predict, and brute force wouldn't be enough to see them through.

She stepped forward, her heart pounding, and placed her hand on the cold stone of the archway. As her fingers brushed the surface, a low, resonant hum echoed through the air, vibrating through her bones. The symbols etched into the stone began to glow faintly, pulsing with a soft, golden light that seemed to breathe with a life of its own.

The ground beneath them trembled, and the fog began to swirl faster, thickening around them until it became almost impossible to see. The air grew heavy, charged with an ancient energy that made the hairs on the back of Lyra's neck stand on end.

And then, from within the shadows beyond the gate, a figure emerged.

At first, it was nothing more than a faint silhouette, barely distinguishable from the swirling fog. But as it stepped closer, the figure began to take shape—a tall, imposing figure clad in gleaming armor, its face hidden behind an ornate helm. The armor was unlike anything Lyra had ever seen, forged from a metal that shimmered with an otherworldly light, as though it had been crafted from the very stars themselves.

In one hand, the figure held a massive sword, its blade glowing with a faint, ethereal light. In the other, it carried a shield emblazoned with intricate symbols that seemed to shift and change with every passing second. The figure radiated power, an ancient and terrifying presence that filled the air with a palpable sense of dread.

The Guardian of the Gate.

Lyra's breath caught in her throat as the figure came to a stop before the archway, its eyes—if it had eyes—fixed on her and her companions. For a long, agonizing moment, no one moved. The only sound was the soft hum of the guardian's armor and the low, rhythmic thrum of the gate behind them.

And then, the guardian spoke.

"Who dares to approach the Gate of Eternity?" the voice was deep, resonant, and carried the weight of ages. It echoed through the fog like the tolling of a distant bell, each word reverberating in Lyra's chest. "Only the worthy may pass beyond this point. The unworthy shall be turned away, or perish."

Sienna stepped forward, her hand resting on the hilt of her dagger, but Lyra held up a hand to stop her. This was not a battle they could win with weapons. The guardian was not an enemy to be defeated with brute force—it was a test, a trial of their resolve, their wisdom, and their worth.

Lyra swallowed hard and stepped forward, her voice steady despite the fear that twisted in her stomach. "We seek the Island of the Immortals," she said, her gaze locked on the towering figure before her. "We have come to prove our worth."

The guardian was silent for a moment, its head tilting slightly as though considering her words. Then, with a slow, deliberate motion, it raised its sword and pointed it at the gate behind them.

"The path you seek lies beyond this gate," the guardian said, its voice low and menacing. "But only those who are worthy may pass. To prove your worth, you must face the trial of the gate. You will be tested—your strength, your courage, your wisdom. And you must solve the riddle that guards this threshold."

"A riddle?" Galen asked, his brow furrowing in confusion.

The guardian nodded, its voice cold and emotionless. "The riddle of the gate is the key to your passage. Fail to answer it, and you shall be denied entry. Succeed, and the gate will open."

Lyra's heart raced. A riddle. She had always been good with puzzles, but this was no ordinary riddle. This was a test from an ancient power, designed to challenge them in ways they couldn't anticipate.

The guardian stepped back, lowering its sword, and the symbols on the gate began to glow brighter, pulsing with a strange, hypnotic light. The air around them grew heavy, and the fog seemed to close in, as though the very island itself was holding its breath, waiting for their response.

The guardian spoke again, its voice echoing through the fog like the toll of a bell.

"Answer me this:

_"I speak without a mouth and hear without ears. I have no body, but I come alive with wind. What am I?"_

The riddle hung in the air, heavy with significance. Lyra's mind raced, trying to piece together the meaning behind the words. It was a riddle of contradictions, of things that existed in one form but not in another. Something that spoke but had no mouth, something that heard but had no ears. Something that was alive with the wind.

Sienna was the first to speak, her voice uncertain. "A spirit?"

The guardian remained silent, its expression unreadable. Lyra shook her head, her brow furrowed in thought. A spirit was too vague, too broad. The riddle was more specific than that.

Galen spoke next, his voice low. "The sea? It moves with the wind, it speaks in waves..."

Again, the guardian gave no response. Lyra felt the pressure mounting, the weight of the trial pressing down on her. If they failed, they would be turned away—perhaps even killed. She had to think, to unravel the layers of meaning behind the words.

"I speak without a mouth and hear without ears," she murmured to herself, her mind working furiously. "I have no body, but I come alive with wind..."

Her eyes widened as the answer struck her like a bolt of lightning.

"The answer is... an echo."

The moment the words left her lips, the air around them seemed to shift. The fog swirled faster, and the symbols on the gate flared with a brilliant, golden light. The guardian, who had remained still and silent, slowly lowered its sword, its head tilting slightly in what might have been approval.

"You have answered correctly," the guardian said, its voice softer now, almost reverent. "An echo speaks without a mouth and hears without ears. It has no body, but it comes alive with the wind."

Lyra let out a breath she hadn't realized she'd been holding. Relief washed over her, but it was short-lived. The trial of the riddle was over, but they were not done yet.

The guardian stepped forward again, its towering figure casting a long shadow over them. "You have proven your wisdom, but the trial is not yet complete. To pass through the gate, you must face your greatest fears. Only then will you be worthy of the path ahead."

Lyra's heart sank. Facing their fears? What did that mean?

Before she could ask, the guardian raised its sword high, and the symbols on the gate began to glow brighter, pulsing with a strange, otherworldly light. The ground beneath them trembled, and the air grew thick with tension. The fog swirled around them, faster and faster, until it felt as though the very island was spinning.

And then, without warning, the world around them seemed to dissolve.

Lyra blinked, disoriented, as the fog lifted. The jagged landscape of the Island of Shadows had disappeared, replaced by something entirely different. She stood alone in a vast, empty field, the sky above her a deep, unnatural shade of red. The air was thick and heavy, and the ground beneath her feet felt strange, almost fluid, as though it could shift at any moment.

She turned in a slow circle, her heart pounding in her chest. Where were the others? Where was the gate? Everything had changed in an instant, and now she was completely alone.

A soft, familiar voice echoed through the air, and Lyra froze. Her breath caught in her throat as the voice grew louder, clearer, until she recognized it.

"Lyra..."

It was her grandmother's voice.

Lyra's heart raced, her pulse quickening as she turned toward the sound. There, standing at the edge of the field, was the figure of her grandmother, the woman who had raised her, who had told her stories of the Island of the Immortals, of the ancient prophecy that had led her here. But her grandmother had been dead for years.

"Grandmother?" Lyra whispered, her voice trembling.

The figure didn't respond. It simply stood there, watching her with sad, hollow eyes. And then, slowly, it began to walk toward her.

Lyra's heart pounded in her chest, a mixture of fear and confusion twisting inside her. This couldn't be real. It had to be an illusion, a trick of the island. But the figure looked so real, so familiar, and as it drew closer, Lyra felt a deep, aching sadness welling up inside her.

"You shouldn't have come here," the figure said, its voice soft and mournful. "This place is not for you, Lyra. You've made a terrible mistake."

Lyra shook her head, backing away. "No... no, this isn't real. You're not real."

The figure tilted its head, its expression filled with sorrow. "I am as real as you are. And I know what you fear most, Lyra. You fear that you will fail. That you will never be worthy of the journey you have begun. You fear that you will end up like me—lost, forgotten, a faded memory in the shadow of this island."

Tears welled up in Lyra's eyes as the figure spoke. The words cut deep, stirring up fears she had buried deep within herself. She had always feared failure, always feared that she wasn't strong enough, smart enough, to complete the quest she had started. And now, those fears were laid bare before her, as real as the figure that stood before her.

"You can't go any further," the figure said, its voice growing colder. "Turn back, Lyra. Turn back before it's too late."

Lyra's heart raced, her mind swirling with doubt. The figure was right—she had doubted herself from the moment they had set sail. She had wondered if she was truly worthy of this journey, if she had the strength to face the trials ahead.

But as the figure reached out to her, its hand cold and lifeless, something inside her snapped.

"No!" Lyra shouted, her voice filled with sudden, fierce determination. "You're wrong. I won't turn back. I've come too far."

The figure hesitated, its eyes narrowing.

"I'm not afraid of failing," Lyra continued, her voice steady and resolute. "I'm afraid of not trying. I'm afraid of giving up before I've even had the chance to prove myself."

The figure's hand wavered, and for a brief moment, its form flickered, like a reflection in a broken mirror.

Lyra took a step forward, her gaze locked on the figure's hollow eyes. "I won't turn back," she said, her voice firm. "I'm not afraid anymore."

The figure's form shimmered, its edges blurring, and then, with a soft sigh, it dissolved into the air, leaving Lyra standing alone in the empty field.

The fog lifted, and the world around her shifted once more. She was back on the Island of Shadows, standing before the gate, the others by her side. They looked disoriented, shaken, but alive.

Lyra's heart pounded as she realized what had just happened. They had each faced their greatest fear, their deepest doubt, and they had survived.

The guardian, still standing before the gate, lowered its sword. "You have faced your fears and proven your worth," it said, its voice softer now. "The path to the Island of the Immortals is open to you."

The gate creaked open, revealing a narrow path that led into the shadows beyond.

Lyra's heart raced with a mixture of fear and anticipation. The trial was over, but the journey was far from complete.

They had passed the test, but the Island of the Immortals still awaited.

End of Chapter 5.

# Chapter 6: The Crossing of the Sea of Mist

The gate behind them groaned shut, its heavy stone doors sealing with a finality that sent a shiver through Lyra. The Island of Shadows was now behind them, but the path ahead seemed no less foreboding. A narrow, rocky trail stretched out before them, winding through the dense fog that blanketed the landscape like a suffocating shroud. Beyond the mist, the sea they had been warned about awaited—the Sea of Mist, a treacherous body of water that distorted reality and played tricks on the mind.

Lyra had read stories about this place, whispered legends passed down through generations. Some spoke of adventurers who had sailed into the mist, only to vanish without a trace, lost in a world where time and space twisted into an unrecognizable labyrinth. Others spoke of sailors who had gone mad, driven to the brink of insanity by the illusions that danced before their eyes. Now, standing on the edge of that very sea, Lyra couldn't help but wonder if they were truly prepared for what awaited them.

She glanced at her companions. Talon stood beside her, his jaw clenched, his eyes fixed on the mist ahead with a mixture of determination and unease. Sienna, ever the pragmatist, had her hand on the hilt of her dagger, her sharp eyes scanning their surroundings as though expecting an ambush at any moment. Galen, though silent, looked tense, his hand resting on the hilt of his sword, while Kael, the most reserved of the group, seemed lost in thought, his brow furrowed in concentration.

"We made it through the gate," Talon said, breaking the silence. His voice was low, steady, but there was an edge of uncertainty to it. "Now we just need to get through this."

Lyra nodded, though she wasn't sure "just" was the right word. The Sea of Mist was unlike any obstacle they had faced so far. The storm had tested their endurance, the Island of Shadows had tested their fears, and the Guardian had tested their worth. But this? This would be something else entirely.

"Let's move forward," Sienna said, her voice firm but quiet. "Standing here won't get us anywhere."

Together, they began to walk, the rocky path beneath their feet slick with moisture from the ever-present fog. The mist was thicker now, swirling around them in thick, ghostly tendrils that clung to their clothing and obscured their vision. Every step forward felt like wading through a dense, impenetrable cloud, and the further they went, the harder it became to see the path ahead.

The trail eventually led them to the shoreline, where the Sea of Mist stretched out before them like a vast, endless expanse of silver-gray water. The surface was eerily calm, almost glassy, and the mist that hovered above it seemed to ripple and shift as though alive. It was a strange, unsettling sight—beautiful in its own way, but filled with a quiet menace that made Lyra's skin crawl.

Sienna, who had taken the lead, stopped at the water's edge and turned to face the group. "We'll need to take the rowboat to cross," she said, her voice steady. "The sea looks calm, but don't be fooled. This place is known for playing tricks on the mind."

Lyra swallowed hard, her gaze fixed on the mist-covered water. She had no idea what to expect once they were out on the sea, but the stories she had heard were enough to make her wary. Illusions. Deception. Madness. The Sea of Mist was infamous for distorting reality, and if they weren't careful, they could easily lose themselves in its treacherous depths.

"Stay close to each other," Lyra said, her voice quiet but firm. "We need to stick together. No matter what we see, no matter what we think we hear, we have to stay focused."

Her companions nodded, each of them understanding the gravity of the situation.

The small rowboat, which had been tied to a nearby dock, looked fragile against the vastness of the sea. Sienna moved quickly to untie it, and they climbed in, one by one, settling onto the narrow wooden seats. The boat rocked gently as it pushed away from the shore, the oars cutting through the mist-covered water with slow, deliberate strokes.

Lyra sat at the front of the boat, her eyes scanning the horizon—or what little of it she could see. The mist was so thick that it was impossible to tell where the sea ended and the sky began. Everything around them was a swirling mass of gray, an endless void that seemed to close in tighter with every passing second.

For a long while, they rowed in silence, the only sound the soft splash of the oars as they cut through the still water. The mist hung heavy around them, muffling even the faintest noises. There was no wind, no birds, no sounds of life—just the oppressive quiet of the Sea of Mist, like a veil separating them from the rest of the world.

The further they ventured, the more disorienting the fog became. The mist twisted and shifted, forming strange shapes in the air, like figures made of smoke dancing just out of reach. Every now and then, Lyra thought she saw something—a shadow, a flicker of movement—but when she blinked, it was gone, swallowed by the fog.

The first sign of trouble came when the sea itself seemed to ripple unnaturally, the water shimmering beneath the surface as though something was moving beneath it. Lyra frowned, her gaze fixed on the spot where the disturbance had occurred, but the water quickly returned to its unnervingly calm state, leaving her to wonder if she had imagined it.

"We should be getting close to the other side," Sienna said, though her voice lacked its usual confidence.

Galen, who had been quiet for most of the journey, finally spoke, his voice low and uneasy. "Do any of you feel like we've been here before?"

Lyra turned to look at him, confusion knitting her brow. "What do you mean?"

Galen shifted uncomfortably in his seat, his hand tightening around the oar. "I don't know. It's just... this feels familiar. Like we're rowing in circles, going nowhere."

Talon glanced at him, his eyes narrowing. "That's just the mist playing tricks on your mind."

But Lyra wasn't so sure. She, too, had started to feel the same strange sense of déjà vu, as though they had been rowing through this sea for much longer than they realized. Time felt distorted here, stretched and twisted in ways that were impossible to understand. It was disorienting, confusing, and more than a little terrifying.

"Keep rowing," she said, her voice tight with determination. "We have to keep moving."

But even as she spoke the words, a creeping doubt began to worm its way into her mind. Were they really moving forward, or had they been rowing in circles all along? The mist made it impossible to tell, and the more she thought about it, the more unsettled she became.

And then, without warning, the sea around them shifted.

The water rippled violently, and the mist began to swirl faster, as though caught in some unseen current. The boat rocked precariously, and Lyra's hand shot out to steady herself as the fog around them thickened, obscuring everything in a dense, suffocating cloud.

"Everyone stay calm!" Sienna shouted, though her voice was edged with panic.

But staying calm was easier said than done. The mist was alive now, swirling around them in thick, choking waves that made it impossible to see more than a few feet in any direction. The boat rocked dangerously, and the water beneath them seemed to come alive, churning and bubbling as though something massive was moving beneath the surface.

Lyra's heart raced, her mind scrambling for some explanation, some way to make sense of what was happening. But there was no logic to the Sea of Mist. Reality itself was bending, twisting in on itself in a way that made her feel as though she was caught in a nightmare from which there was no escape.

"Lyra, look!" Talon's voice cut through the chaos, drawing her attention to the water beside the boat.

Lyra's breath caught in her throat as she saw what he was pointing at.

Beneath the surface of the mist-covered sea, dark shapes moved, their forms shadowy and indistinct, like figures trapped beneath a sheet of glass. They moved in slow, languid motions, their shapes flickering in and out of focus as the water rippled and churned around them.

And then, one of the figures broke the surface.

Lyra gasped, her hand flying to her mouth as a pale, translucent figure emerged from the water, its eyes hollow and empty, its body shimmering like a reflection in a pool of still water. The figure floated just above the surface of the sea, its mouth moving soundlessly as though it were trying to speak.

"It's a trick," Sienna said, her voice tight with fear. "It's an illusion. Don't look at it."

But Lyra couldn't tear her eyes away. There was something hauntingly familiar about the figure, something that tugged at her heart in a way she couldn't explain. And then, in a flash of realization, she knew.

The figure hovering above the water... it was her.

Lyra stared in horror at the ghostly reflection of herself, her heart pounding in her chest. The translucent figure mirrored her exactly, from the shape of her face to the clothes she wore. It was as though she was looking at a version of herself that had been lost to the sea, a version of herself that had never made it this far.

"What... what is this?" she whispered, her voice trembling.

"It's you," the figure said, its voice soft and distant, like an echo carried on the wind. "Or rather, it's the version of you that could have been."

Lyra's blood ran cold. The version of her that could have been? What did that mean?

"You could have turned back," the figure continued, its eyes fixed on hers. "You could have stayed safe, in your village, living an ordinary life. You didn't have to come here. You didn't have to risk everything."

Lyra's breath caught in her throat. The words hit her like a punch to the gut, stirring up doubts and fears she had tried to bury deep within herself. She had always known that this journey would be dangerous, but now, faced with this ghostly reflection of herself, she couldn't help but wonder... had she made the right choice?

"You could have lived a peaceful life," the figure said, its voice filled with quiet regret. "You could have been happy. But now... look at where you are. Lost in the Sea of Mist, with no way forward and no way back."

Lyra's heart raced, her mind spinning with confusion and doubt. The figure was right. She could have stayed behind. She could have chosen safety, chosen the life she had known. But instead, she had chosen this—a journey into the unknown, a quest for something that might not even exist.

"I..." Lyra faltered, her voice barely a whisper. "I had to do this. I had to find the island."

"Why?" the figure asked, its empty eyes boring into hers. "Why risk everything? Why chase after something that might not be real?"

The question hung in the air, heavy with significance.

Why?

Lyra had asked herself that question a thousand times since they had set sail. Why had she chosen this path? Why had she decided to seek the Island of the Immortals, knowing the dangers that lay ahead? Was it for the promise of immortality, the chance to live forever? Or was it something deeper, something she couldn't quite put into words?

"I don't know," she whispered, her voice trembling. "I don't know why."

The figure's expression softened, and for a brief moment, it almost looked... sad. "That's the problem, Lyra. You don't know why. And until you figure it out, you'll never escape this place. You'll be trapped here, lost in the mist, just like me."

Lyra's heart clenched, her mind reeling with the weight of the words. Trapped. Lost. She had always feared losing her way, feared that she would never find the answers she was looking for. And now, faced with this ghostly reflection of herself, those fears felt more real than ever.

But as she stared into the hollow eyes of the figure, something inside her shifted.

No.

She wasn't going to let this illusion, this trick of the Sea of Mist, get the better of her. She had come too far to turn back now, too far to give in to the doubts and fears that had haunted her since the beginning of this journey.

"I don't know why I'm here," Lyra said, her voice growing stronger. "But that doesn't mean I'm going to stop. I'm not afraid of the unknown, and I'm not going to let my fear keep me from moving forward."

The figure blinked, its hollow eyes widening in surprise.

"I don't have all the answers yet," Lyra continued, her voice steady. "But I'm going to keep searching. I'm going to keep pushing forward, no matter what. And I'm not going to let you—or anything else—stop me."

For a moment, the figure said nothing. And then, slowly, it began to fade, its form dissolving into the mist like smoke caught in the wind.

Lyra let out a breath she hadn't realized she'd been holding, her heart racing in her chest.

The mist around them began to lift, the swirling clouds thinning as the boat pushed forward. The water beneath them grew calm once more, and the dark shapes that had been lurking beneath the surface vanished, leaving only the still, quiet sea behind.

Lyra turned to her companions, her breath still ragged from the encounter. She could see the confusion and fear in their eyes—they had seen things too, faced their own illusions, their own doubts and insecurities. But they had survived.

They had crossed the Sea of Mist.

"We're through," Sienna said, her voice soft but filled with relief. "We made it."

Lyra nodded, her gaze drifting to the horizon, where the outline of an island began to take shape in the distance.

The Island of the Immortals was close.

But the hardest part of their journey was yet to come.

End of Chapter 6.

# Chapter 7: The Land of Eternal Youth

The silhouette of the island slowly emerged from the mist like a mirage, a shimmering oasis in an endless sea of uncertainty. Lyra could hardly believe they had made it. The Island of the Immortals—the place of legend, the elusive paradise promised in stories whispered around firesides—was finally before them.

As the mist began to lift, revealing the island in all its grandeur, the first thing Lyra noticed was the vibrant, almost otherworldly beauty that stretched before them. Lush greenery covered the hills, with towering trees that seemed to sparkle with dew even in the warm sunlight. Flowers in shades she had never seen before—colors too rich, too brilliant to belong to the world she knew—bloomed along the shoreline. The air was warm and sweet, carrying a faint, intoxicating scent that made Lyra feel lightheaded as they approached.

She glanced at her companions. Sienna's sharp eyes, usually hard with suspicion, softened as she took in the beauty of the island. Talon's usual wariness seemed to slip away, his face slack with awe. Galen, who had been silent since their ordeal on the Sea of Mist, now breathed deeply, as if he were savoring the very air of this place. Even Kael, ever the skeptic, looked momentarily entranced, his usual tension giving way to quiet wonder.

"This is it," Lyra whispered, her voice barely audible as they neared the shore. "The Island of the Immortals."

The rowboat glided effortlessly over the calm, crystalline waters, the tension of the Sea of Mist now a distant memory. As they stepped ashore, the sand beneath their boots felt impossibly soft, warm as if kissed by eternal sunlight. The sea lapped gently at the beach, and just beyond, the forest beckoned, its trees swaying gently in the breeze, as if alive with a secret rhythm.

The group stood in silence for a moment, taking in the splendor of the island. There was no sign of decay here, no imperfection—everything felt pure, untouched by time.

"This place," Sienna murmured, shaking her head as though she couldn't quite believe what she was seeing. "It's like a dream."

Galen nodded, his eyes wide. "No, it's like paradise."

Lyra's chest swelled with hope, but beneath that hope, a flicker of unease tugged at the back of her mind. The island was too perfect. Too serene. She had expected something different—something more... challenging. They had faced so many trials just to get here, but now that they had arrived, it felt almost too easy.

Before she could voice her concerns, a soft sound drifted through the air—a melody, gentle and haunting, carried on the breeze. Lyra turned toward the sound and saw them.

The inhabitants of the island.

They came from the forest, moving with a grace that was both unnatural and mesmerizing. There were about a dozen of them, their faces serene, their bodies ageless. The women wore flowing robes of silk that shimmered in the sunlight, while the men were dressed in tunics of fine cloth, their features perfect, as if carved by the gods themselves. They walked barefoot across the sand, their movements fluid, as though they were gliding rather than walking. Their eyes sparkled with an ageless wisdom, and yet, there was something... distant about them.

Lyra's breath caught in her throat. These were the immortals—those who had transcended the boundaries of life and death, those who had lived for centuries, perhaps millennia, on this island untouched by time. Their beauty was overwhelming, almost painful to look at.

The group of immortals stopped a short distance from Lyra and her companions, their expressions welcoming but unreadable. The leader, a tall man with hair the color of molten gold and eyes as blue as the clearest summer sky, stepped forward and inclined his head in greeting.

"Welcome, travelers," he said, his voice smooth and melodic. "You have made a long and difficult journey to reach us. Few have come this far, and fewer still have proven worthy."

Lyra swallowed, her heart racing. "Are you... the immortals?"

The man smiled, though the expression didn't quite reach his eyes. "We are the Guardians of the Island of Eternal Youth. And you," he gestured to the group, "are among the few who have reached this sacred place."

Behind him, the other immortals watched silently, their eyes fixed on Lyra and her companions with an intensity that made her skin crawl. They were beautiful, yes, but there was something unnerving about them—something that made Lyra feel like she was being studied, evaluated.

The leader stepped closer, his gaze settling on Lyra. "You have come seeking immortality, have you not?"

Lyra hesitated, unsure of how to answer. Had she truly come seeking immortality? The question seemed more complicated now, standing in the presence of those who had achieved it.

Talon, ever the pragmatist, stepped forward, his voice steady. "We've come to find the truth about this place. We've heard the legends, the stories of eternal life. But we want to know... what's the price?"

The immortal's smile widened, but there was no warmth in it. "Ah, yes. The price. There is always a price, isn't there?"

He gestured to the island around them. "Look at this place. It is paradise. Here, time stands still. The sun never sets, the seasons never change. We live in eternal youth, free from the ravages of age and sickness. Our bodies remain as they are, perfect and unchanging."

Galen's eyes lit up with awe. "You mean... we could live forever? Just like you?"

"Yes," the leader said, his voice soft and alluring. "You could. You could remain here, ageless and immortal, untouched by the passage of time."

Lyra's heart skipped a beat. It sounded too good to be true. Eternal life. Eternal youth. The very thing so many had sought for centuries.

But then, as she looked into the eyes of the immortal, she saw it—something cold, something hidden beneath the surface.

"And what's the cost?" she asked, her voice quiet but firm. "What do we have to give up?"

The immortal's smile faltered, and for the first time, a flicker of something dark crossed his face.

"Immortality comes with a price, as all things do," he said, his voice dropping to a near whisper. "To live forever, you must give up your memories of the mortal world. Everything you were, everything you loved, everything you have known—it will all fade away. Your past will be wiped clean, and you will become one with the island, one with eternity."

Lyra's stomach dropped. Her memories? She would have to give up her memories?

Beside her, Sienna stiffened, her hand tightening on the hilt of her dagger. "You mean we'd have to forget who we are?"

"Yes," the leader said simply. "Your mortal life will become a distant dream, forgotten in the mists of eternity. You will become something greater—something eternal. But to do so, you must leave behind everything that ties you to the world of mortals."

Lyra's mind raced, her heart pounding in her chest. Her memories—everything she had experienced, everything she had fought for, everything that made her who she was—she would have to give it all up to gain immortality.

She thought of her grandmother, the woman who had raised her, who had told her stories of the island, who had planted the seed of adventure in her heart. She thought of the village she had left behind, the people she had known, the life she had lived. Could she really give all that up?

Talon's voice broke through her thoughts. "So we'd have to forget everything? Our families, our friends, our lives?"

"Yes," the immortal said, his gaze steady. "Your mortal ties will be severed. But in return, you will gain something far greater—eternity."

Kael, who had been silent for most of the exchange, finally spoke, his voice laced with disbelief. "And what happens if we refuse? What if we don't want to give up our memories?"

The leader's smile returned, but this time, it was colder, more calculating. "If you choose to leave, you may. The island will not force you to stay. But know this—those who leave can never return. And the passage back to the mortal world is fraught with danger. Many have tried to leave and failed."

Lyra's heart raced. This was the moment they had been working toward, the moment when they would decide whether to take the gift of immortality or to return to their mortal lives. But now that the choice was before her, it didn't feel like a gift at all. It felt like a trap.

"I don't want to forget," Lyra said, her voice trembling slightly. "I don't want to lose who I am."

The leader's gaze darkened, and for a moment, the serene facade of the immortals slipped. "That is the choice you must make. To live forever, you must become one with the island. You must let go of the mortal world and all that it holds."

Talon stepped closer to Lyra, his expression hard. "We've been through too much to let it all go now. Our memories, our past—they're what make us who we are."

Sienna nodded, her hand still on her dagger. "I'm not giving up my life for some hollow version of eternity."

Galen, who had been so enthralled by the idea of immortality, now looked torn, his brow furrowed in confusion. "But... what if this is the only chance we have? To live forever? To escape death?"

Kael shook his head, his voice quiet but resolute. "Living forever without memories isn't living. It's existing. It's losing everything that makes you human."

Lyra's mind whirled with confusion and doubt. The promise of immortality had drawn them here, but now that it was within reach, it felt like a terrible choice. Could she really give up everything she had known, everything she had fought for, just to live forever?

The leader of the immortals stepped closer, his expression softening slightly. "I understand your hesitation. But you must ask yourselves—what is more important? The fleeting moments of your mortal life, or the eternal peace that awaits you here?"

Lyra's heart clenched. The fleeting moments of her mortal life. That was what it came down to, wasn't it? Her life, her memories, her experiences—they were fleeting, temporary, destined to fade away with time. But they were hers. They were what made her who she was.

She thought of her grandmother's words, the stories she had told of the Island of the Immortals. "Be careful what you seek," her grandmother had said. "For sometimes, the price is greater than you can imagine."

And now, standing on the edge of eternity, Lyra understood what her grandmother had meant.

She turned to her companions, her voice steady but filled with emotion. "I don't want to forget. I don't want to lose everything that makes me who I am. I would rather live a mortal life, with all its pain and joy, than spend eternity as a shadow of myself."

Talon nodded, his gaze filled with fierce determination. "I'm with you, Lyra. I won't give up who I am for this."

Sienna's eyes were hard, her voice laced with conviction. "I didn't fight through hell just to forget everything I've been through. I'll take my chances in the mortal world."

Galen hesitated, his eyes flicking between the immortals and his companions. For a moment, it looked like he might be swayed by the promise of eternal youth, but then he sighed, his shoulders sagging. "You're right. Living forever means nothing if you forget who you are. I'm with you."

Kael, ever the quiet voice of reason, simply nodded, his gaze resolute. "We leave together."

The leader of the immortals watched them in silence, his expression unreadable. Then, slowly, he nodded. "Very well. You have made your choice."

He stepped aside, gesturing toward the forest behind him. "The way out lies through the heart of the island. But be warned—the path back is not easy. The island will not let you go so easily."

Lyra's heart pounded as she turned to face the dense forest that loomed before them. The island was beautiful, yes, but now it felt like a cage, a gilded prison that would not release them without a fight.

"We're ready," Lyra said, her voice firm.

The leader nodded once, his expression unreadable. "Then may the gods be with you."

Without another word, Lyra and her companions turned and began their journey into the heart of the island, leaving the immortals and their empty promises behind.

The path ahead was uncertain, fraught with danger. But Lyra knew one thing for sure—she would not give up her memories, her life, her humanity, for anything. Not even for eternity.

End of Chapter 7.

# Chapter 8: The Council of Immortals

The path through the heart of the island was a winding labyrinth of towering trees and dense foliage, illuminated by shafts of golden sunlight that filtered through the canopy above. Despite the beauty that surrounded them, there was a growing sense of unease that settled over Lyra and her companions as they walked. The promise of eternal life had lost its luster after their encounter with the ageless inhabitants at the shore. The island, with all its allure, now felt like a place where nothing was what it seemed.

The air grew thicker as they made their way deeper into the forest, the scent of the flowers and plants around them almost too sweet, too cloying. It was as if the island itself was alive, watching their every move, waiting for them to make their next choice.

"We should be getting close," Sienna said, her voice cutting through the heavy silence that had fallen over the group. Her sharp eyes scanned the path ahead, but even she seemed unsettled by the oppressive atmosphere.

"Close to what?" Galen muttered under his breath, his hand gripping the hilt of his sword tightly. "Another trap? Another test?"

"No," Lyra said quietly, though she wasn't entirely sure. "We're headed for the Council. The immortals said they would show us the truth of this place."

"The truth," Talon scoffed. "If that's what we're after, we should be careful. Truths here come with a price."

Lyra didn't respond, but she felt the weight of his words. They had faced trials of endurance, fear, and self-deception. Now, as they prepared to meet the mysterious Council of Immortals, she knew they would be asked to make a final choice—one that would define the rest of their lives.

The forest began to thin as they neared a clearing, the trees parting to reveal a wide, open space. At the center of the clearing stood a massive stone structure, unlike anything Lyra had ever seen before. It was a circular building, its walls carved with intricate symbols and runes that seemed to pulse faintly with an inner light. The stone itself was smooth and polished, gleaming in the sunlight like marble, though it was far older than any mortal structure.

As they approached the entrance, two towering figures emerged from the shadows, their bodies clad in the same shimmering armor as the guardian they had encountered at the gate. These were no ordinary guards—they were immortals, their faces impassive, their eyes glowing faintly with a cold, otherworldly light.

Without a word, the guards motioned for the group to follow them inside.

Lyra's heart pounded as they stepped through the entrance and into the chamber beyond. The interior of the structure was vast, with high, vaulted ceilings that seemed to stretch up into infinity. The walls were lined with more of the glowing runes, casting a soft, golden light over the room.

At the far end of the chamber, seated on a raised dais, were five figures. The Council of Immortals.

They were unlike the other immortals Lyra had encountered. These beings radiated a presence that was both awe-inspiring and terrifying. Each one wore a long robe of shimmering fabric that seemed to change color with every movement, and their faces were serene, almost otherworldly. Their eyes, glowing faintly like the runes on the walls, seemed to pierce through the very soul.

The leader of the council, a tall figure with long, silver hair and skin so pale it seemed to glow, stood as Lyra and her companions approached. His voice, when he spoke, was like the soft rustle of leaves in the wind, but it carried a power that sent a shiver down Lyra's spine.

"Welcome, travelers," he said, his gaze sweeping over the group. "You have come far, endured much, and proven yourselves worthy to stand before the Council of Immortals."

Lyra felt her heart race in her chest. Worthy. The word hung in the air, heavy with significance. But worthy of what?

"You seek immortality," the leader continued, his eyes locking onto Lyra's. "But do you understand what it truly means?"

Lyra swallowed hard, her mind racing. She had come here seeking answers, seeking the truth about the Island of the Immortals. But now, standing before the council, she realized she didn't know what to expect.

The leader gestured to the other council members, who rose from their seats and stepped forward. Each one carried an air of immense wisdom and power, their eyes filled with centuries of knowledge.

"The immortality you seek is not simply the preservation of the body," one of the council members said, a woman with hair the color of midnight and eyes like burning embers. "It is the transcendence of the self. To become immortal is to shed the limitations of mortality—not just physically, but spiritually."

"To live forever," another council member added, his voice low and resonant, "is not simply to exist without death. It is to exist beyond the boundaries of time and space, beyond the constraints of the mortal mind."

Lyra's breath caught in her throat. The words were beautiful, but they also carried a weight that made her feel small, insignificant in the face of such vast knowledge.

"And yet," the leader of the council said softly, his gaze never leaving hers, "immortality comes with a price."

Lyra nodded. She had known this from the beginning. Everything came with a price.

The leader's eyes darkened, and his voice dropped to a near whisper. "To transcend mortality, you must be willing to let go of everything that ties you to the mortal world. Your memories, your past, your sense of self—all must be relinquished."

The words hit Lyra like a punch to the gut. She had heard this before, but now, standing before the council, it felt more real, more terrifying. To live forever, she would have to give up everything that made her who she was.

Sienna stepped forward, her voice hard. "So we have to forget everything? Our lives, our families? Why? What does that accomplish?"

The council members exchanged a glance, their faces unreadable.

"Immortality," the woman with midnight hair said, "is not merely the extension of life. It is the transformation of the soul. To hold on to the past, to cling to the memories of a mortal existence, is to remain bound by the limitations of that existence. To become immortal, you must become something more."

"Something more?" Talon scoffed. "You mean, something less human?"

The leader of the council nodded slowly. "Yes. Immortality is not for those who wish to remain human. It is for those who wish to transcend the human condition."

Kael, who had been silent for much of the journey, stepped forward, his brow furrowed in thought. "And what happens to those who choose not to transcend? Those who decide they don't want to give up their memories, their humanity?"

The council's leader regarded him for a long moment before answering. "Those who choose not to transcend are free to leave. The island does not force its gifts upon anyone. But know this—the choice is final. Once you leave, you cannot return."

Lyra's mind raced. The promise of immortality had seemed so alluring at first, but now, faced with the reality of what it entailed, she wasn't so sure. Could she really give up everything that made her who she was? Could she really forget her past, her memories, her loved ones?

And if she chose to leave, what would that mean for her future? Could she ever go back to her old life, knowing what she had seen, knowing what she had given up?

The leader of the council seemed to sense her inner turmoil and stepped closer, his eyes softening. "Immortality is not for everyone. It is a choice, a sacrifice that must be made willingly. But know this—those who choose to transcend will become part of something greater than themselves. They will become one with the island, one with eternity."

Galen, who had been silent since their arrival, suddenly spoke, his voice filled with confusion and doubt. "But what does that mean? To become part of the island? Are we just... giving up who we are for some vague promise of eternity?"

The leader of the council regarded him for a moment, his expression unreadable. "To become part of the island is to become one with the eternal flow of life and death, to exist beyond the physical and the spiritual. It is to become something more than mortal, something beyond time and space."

"But we would lose ourselves," Galen said, his voice trembling. "We would lose everything that makes us who we are."

"Yes," the leader said softly. "But in losing yourself, you would gain something far greater—eternity."

The chamber fell silent, the weight of the council's words hanging heavy in the air. Each of them—Lyra, Talon, Sienna, Galen, and Kael—stood in the presence of immortality, faced with a choice that would define the rest of their existence.

Lyra's mind raced, her heart pounding in her chest. She thought of her grandmother, the woman who had told her stories of the island, who had sparked the fire of adventure in her heart. She thought of the village she had left behind, the people she had known, the life she had lived. Could she really give all that up?

"I don't want to forget," Lyra said, her voice barely above a whisper. "I don't want to lose who I am."

The leader of the council's gaze softened, and for a moment, he looked almost sad. "The choice is yours to make. Immortality is not for everyone."

Talon stepped forward, his expression hard. "I'm not interested in giving up my memories for some promise of eternity. My life—my memories—are worth more than that."

Sienna nodded, her eyes sharp. "I didn't fight through hell just to forget everything I've been through. I'm not giving up my humanity."

Kael, ever the quiet voice of reason, simply shook his head. "Immortality without memory is meaningless."

Galen hesitated, his eyes flicking between the council and his companions. For a moment, it looked like he might be swayed by the promise of eternal life, but then he sighed, his shoulders sagging. "You're right. Living forever means nothing if you forget who you are. I'm with you."

The leader of the council nodded, his expression calm but unreadable. "Very well. You have made your choice."

He gestured to the chamber around them. "The way out lies through the heart of the island. But be warned—the path back is not easy. The island will not let you go so easily."

Lyra's heart pounded as she turned to face the forest that loomed beyond the chamber. The island was beautiful, yes, but now it felt like a prison, a place that would not release them without a fight.

"We're ready," Lyra said, her voice firm.

The council members stepped aside, their eyes watching in silence as Lyra and her companions turned and made their way toward the exit. The path ahead was uncertain, fraught with danger, but Lyra knew one thing for sure—she would not give up her memories, her life, her humanity, for anything. Not even for eternity.

As they stepped out into the forest, the air felt different—heavier, more oppressive. The island was watching them, waiting for them to make their move. And Lyra knew that the final trial was yet to come.

But they were ready.

End of Chapter 8.

# Chapter 9: The Forbidden Knowledge

The forest closed in around them as Lyra and her companions moved deeper into the island's heart, the air thick with an oppressive stillness that made every sound seem distant and muffled. There was something different now, something darker than when they had first arrived. The beauty of the island, once captivating, now felt like a mask concealing something far more sinister beneath the surface.

Lyra's thoughts swirled as they made their way through the dense foliage, her mind still grappling with the Council of Immortals' words. Immortality was no longer the shimmering promise it had once been; it was a burden, a curse that came at too high a cost. She couldn't shake the feeling that there was more to the story than what the council had revealed. The air hummed with secrets—secrets that the island itself seemed desperate to keep hidden.

As they walked, the trees began to thin, and the path ahead opened up into a small clearing. In the center of the clearing stood a stone structure, half-hidden by the overgrowth of vines and thick vegetation. The structure was ancient, far older than the gleaming, polished stone of the council chamber. Its surface was rough and weathered, worn down by centuries of wind and rain. There was a sense of deep history here, as though this place had been forgotten by time, left to decay beneath the weight of the island's secrets.

"What is this?" Sienna muttered, stepping forward to inspect the crumbling structure.

"I don't know," Lyra replied, her voice barely above a whisper. "But I think we're meant to find it."

Galen knelt beside the stone entrance, his brow furrowed in concentration. "It looks like a tomb. Or maybe a temple of some kind. Whatever it is, it's old. Older than anything we've seen on this island."

Talon, ever the pragmatist, ran his hand along the rough stone, his eyes narrowed. "Why would the immortals let this place fall into ruin? If they're so powerful, why leave something like this behind?"

Lyra stepped closer to the entrance, her gaze drawn to the faded symbols carved into the stone. The markings were different from the ones she had seen on the council chamber—these were older, more primitive, yet they pulsed faintly with the same golden light that had illuminated the runes inside the gate. There was power here, ancient and forgotten, but still alive.

"We need to go inside," Lyra said, her voice steady but filled with a growing sense of urgency. "There's something here, something the council didn't tell us. I can feel it."

Sienna glanced at her, skeptical but willing to follow. "You think this is the key to the island's secrets?"

"I don't just think it," Lyra replied, her heart racing. "I know it."

Without waiting for further discussion, Lyra stepped forward and pushed against the heavy stone door. It groaned in protest, but after a moment, it gave way, swinging open to reveal a dark, narrow passage that led deep into the earth. A faint, musty smell wafted from the entrance, the air inside cool and stale, as though it hadn't been disturbed in centuries.

Galen lit a torch, its flickering flame casting long shadows across the stone walls as they descended into the chamber below. The passage was narrow and steep, the walls lined with more of the ancient carvings that seemed to shift and pulse with an eerie, otherworldly light.

As they reached the bottom of the stairs, the passage opened up into a vast underground chamber. The walls were lined with shelves, and on those shelves were hundreds of scrolls, each one carefully rolled and tied with brittle, yellowing string. Ancient artifacts—swords, shields, jewelry—lay scattered across the stone floor, covered in dust and cobwebs. There was a sense of decay here, of something long abandoned, yet preserved by time.

Lyra's heart pounded in her chest as she took it all in. This was it. This was what they had been searching for—the hidden history of the island, the truth behind the immortals and the curse of eternal life.

"Look at this," Kael said, his voice hushed with awe as he knelt to inspect one of the scrolls. "These writings are thousands of years old."

Lyra moved toward the center of the chamber, her eyes scanning the rows of scrolls and artifacts. There was a sense of power here, but it wasn't the same kind of power she had felt in the council chamber. This was different, darker, as though the very walls of the chamber were alive with the knowledge they held.

"What do you think this place was?" Talon asked, his voice filled with curiosity as he picked up an ancient sword, its blade dull with age.

"It was a library," Lyra said, her voice soft but certain. "A place where the immortals kept their most precious knowledge. Before they became what they are now."

Sienna, who had been inspecting one of the shelves, turned to face Lyra, her brow furrowed. "What do you mean? What were they before?"

Lyra took a deep breath, her mind racing as she pieced together the fragments of history she had uncovered. "The immortals weren't always like this. They were once like us—mortal. This island wasn't always a place of eternal life. It was a place of balance, of harmony between life and death. The people who lived here understood the natural cycle of life. But something changed."

Kael, who had been carefully examining one of the scrolls, looked up at her, his eyes wide. "You think the thirst for immortality destroyed that balance?"

Lyra nodded, her heart heavy with the weight of the realization. "Yes. The people who lived here, the ones who became the immortals—they sought to transcend death. They wanted to live forever. But in doing so, they upset the balance. The island was never meant to grant eternal life. It was meant to be a place where life and death coexisted in harmony."

"And now they're trapped," Sienna said, her voice filled with quiet understanding. "The immortals are bound to the island, cursed by their own desire for power."

Lyra moved toward the back of the chamber, where a large stone pedestal stood in the center of the room. On the pedestal lay a single scroll, larger and more ornate than the others. It was bound with golden thread, the edges of the parchment glowing faintly with the same ethereal light that pulsed through the carvings on the walls.

"This is it," Lyra whispered, her hand trembling as she reached for the scroll. "This is the key."

She untied the golden thread and unrolled the scroll carefully, her eyes scanning the ancient symbols that lined the parchment. As she read, the truth of the island unfolded before her, each word revealing the dark history that had been hidden for centuries.

The island, she learned, had once been a sanctuary for those seeking peace and knowledge. The people who lived here had been scholars, healers, and mystics—dedicated to understanding the mysteries of life and death. They believed that life was a cycle, a continuous flow of energy that moved between birth and death, and they sought to live in harmony with that cycle.

But as their knowledge grew, so did their ambition. Some among them began to question the inevitability of death. They believed that with enough power, they could break free from the cycle and achieve immortality. They began to experiment with ancient magic, tapping into the very essence of life itself in their quest to escape death.

At first, their experiments seemed successful. They discovered ways to extend their lives, to preserve their youth and vitality. But the magic they had unleashed came with a terrible price. The more they sought to escape death, the more they became bound to the island. Their bodies stopped aging, but their souls were trapped, unable to move on to the next stage of existence.

Over time, the island itself began to change. The balance between life and death was disrupted, and the island became a place of stagnation, a prison for those who had sought immortality. The people who had once lived in harmony with the natural cycle were now bound to the island, their memories fading, their identities lost. They had become the immortals—ageless, but trapped in an eternal limbo.

Lyra's heart sank as she finished reading the scroll. This was the truth the council had not told them. The immortals were not gods. They were prisoners—trapped by their own greed, their own fear of death. And now, they were offering the same cursed gift to anyone who sought it.

"We were right," Lyra said, her voice shaking with emotion as she looked up at her companions. "The immortals are trapped. They sought eternal life, but they've lost everything that made them human. Their memories, their identities, their souls—they've given it all up for the promise of living forever."

Talon's face darkened, his hand tightening around the hilt of his sword. "And now they want us to do the same."

"They're not offering us immortality," Kael said, his voice filled with quiet anger. "They're offering us a prison. A life without death, without memories, without meaning."

Sienna crossed her arms, her expression hard. "So what do we do now? We can't stay here, but we can't just leave without doing something."

Lyra stared down at the scroll in her hands, the weight of the island's history pressing down on her. She had come here seeking answers, but now that she had them, she wasn't sure what to do. The immortals were powerful, yes, but they were also victims of their own ambition. They had lost everything in their pursuit of eternal life, and now they were offering the same fate to others.

"We need to get out of here," Lyra said, her voice steady but filled with resolve. "But we can't leave the island the way it is. We need to break the cycle."

Galen frowned, his brow furrowed in confusion. "Break the cycle? How?"

Lyra took a deep breath, her mind racing as she pieced together the fragments of knowledge she had uncovered. "The island is trapped in a state of stagnation because the immortals disrupted the natural cycle of life and death. If we can restore that balance, if we can find a way to free the island from the magic that binds it, the immortals will be released. They'll finally be able to move on."

"But how do we do that?" Kael asked, his voice tinged with doubt. "We're just mortals. What can we do against magic this powerful?"

Lyra looked down at the scroll in her hands, the ancient symbols glowing faintly in the dim light of the chamber. "There has to be a way," she said softly. "This scroll—this knowledge—was left here for a reason. The people who once lived here, before they became the immortals, must have known there was a way to undo what had been done."

Sienna stepped forward, her voice low and steady. "If there's a way to break the cycle, we'll find it. But we have to be careful. The council won't let us go easily."

Lyra nodded, her heart pounding with a mixture of fear and determination. They had uncovered the truth of the island, but now they had to act. The immortals had offered them a false promise, but Lyra wasn't willing to accept it—not when there was a chance to set things right.

"We need to leave this chamber," Lyra said, rolling up the scroll and tucking it carefully into her pack. "We need to confront the council, but we can't do it alone. We need to find a way to weaken the magic that binds them."

Talon's eyes narrowed, his jaw set with determination. "Then let's get out of here and figure out how to do that."

Together, they made their way back up the narrow passage, their minds filled with the weight of what they had uncovered. The island was no longer the paradise they had once believed it to be—it was a prison, and the immortals were its most tragic victims.

But Lyra was determined to free them. To restore the balance that had been lost so long ago.

As they stepped out of the chamber and into the fading light of the island's forest, Lyra felt a renewed sense of purpose. The island's secrets had been revealed, and now it was up to them to decide what to do with that knowledge.

They were no longer just seeking immortality—they were fighting to restore the natural order. To break the cycle of greed and power that had cursed this place for centuries.

And they would not stop until the island was free.

End of Chapter 9.

# Chapter 10: The Curse of Immortality

Lyra felt the weight of the scroll in her pack as they trudged through the thick, vine-covered forest. The revelation of the immortals' fate and the island's dark past weighed heavily on her mind, and she couldn't shake the feeling that they were entangled in something far bigger and more dangerous than they had imagined. The lush beauty of the island had been deceptive from the start, masking the deep-rooted curse that bound it and its inhabitants. Now that she knew the truth, the island felt less like a paradise and more like a gilded prison.

As they walked, Sienna moved up beside her, breaking the silence that had fallen over the group since they had left the hidden chamber.

"What do you think we'll find?" Sienna asked, her voice low, cautious.

Lyra shook her head, glancing around at the towering trees that seemed to close in on them. "I don't know," she admitted, her brow furrowing. "But the more we learn, the more I'm certain this place isn't what it appears to be. The immortals are prisoners here, bound by their own desire for eternal life. They can't leave, Sienna. They're stuck here, trapped in this cycle. Immortality isn't a gift—it's a curse."

Sienna sighed, her sharp gaze scanning the path ahead. "I've had a feeling from the moment we set foot on this island that something was off. It's too perfect, too quiet. And the way the immortals act... like they're not even human anymore."

"They aren't," Lyra said quietly. "Not really. Not in the way we are."

As they pressed on, Lyra's thoughts returned to the scroll she had found in the hidden chamber. The knowledge it contained was both enlightening and terrifying. The story of how the immortals had once been like them, mortal beings who had lived in harmony with the natural cycle of life and death, was haunting. They had sought to escape death, to transcend their mortal limitations, but in doing so, they had severed themselves from the cycle of life. And now, they were trapped, bound to the island by the very magic they had used to achieve immortality.

As they walked, Lyra could feel the presence of the island all around them. The trees seemed to whisper, the air thick with an ancient energy that made her skin prickle. She had always known that the island was more than just a place—it was alive, in a way that was difficult to explain. But now, with the knowledge of the curse that bound the immortals to this land, the island felt oppressive, as though it was watching their every move, waiting for them to make their next mistake.

"Do you think they'll try to stop us?" Galen asked, breaking the silence as he glanced over his shoulder, his hand resting on the hilt of his sword. "The council, I mean. Now that we know the truth?"

Lyra nodded, her jaw tightening. "They have to. They've spent centuries keeping the secret of their curse hidden. If we try to leave or expose the truth, they won't let us go without a fight."

Kael, walking behind Galen, frowned. "But why keep the secret? What's the point of trapping more people in this curse? Don't they want to be free too?"

"I think," Lyra said slowly, "that the immortals have forgotten what it means to be free. They've been trapped here for so long, bound to the island and to each other, that they've lost their humanity. They don't remember what it means to live and die, to experience the passage of time. All they know now is existence. And they want others to share that existence, because they fear being alone."

Talon, who had been silent for much of the conversation, finally spoke, his voice grim. "Or maybe they want power. Immortality gives them control over this island, over everyone who comes here. They're not interested in freedom—they're interested in maintaining their rule."

Lyra considered his words, her mind racing. He wasn't wrong. The council had made it clear that they were the ones who governed the island, who decided who was worthy of immortality and who was not. But now that she knew the truth, Lyra wondered if their rule was as absolute as it appeared.

"Whatever their motives," Lyra said, "we have to find a way to break the curse. If we don't, we'll be trapped here just like them."

The group fell into a tense silence as they continued walking, the oppressive weight of the island's curse hanging over them. Lyra's thoughts churned with the gravity of their situation. The immortals had sought eternal life but had only found eternal imprisonment. They could not die, but they could not leave the island either. It was a prison of their own making, and now Lyra and her companions stood on the precipice of falling into the same trap.

As they reached the edge of a steep ravine, the forest gave way to a series of jagged cliffs that overlooked a vast, shimmering lake. The water was unnaturally still, its surface like glass, reflecting the sky above. It was beautiful, but there was an eerie stillness to it that made Lyra's skin crawl.

"Look," Sienna said, pointing across the lake.

On the far side of the water, nestled against the cliffs, was a large stone structure—another ancient temple or shrine, but this one far more elaborate than the hidden chamber they had discovered earlier. Its walls were adorned with intricate carvings, and at the center of the temple stood a massive stone archway, its surface glowing faintly with the same golden light that had marked the other ruins they had seen.

Lyra's heart quickened. This was it. This was where they would find the final piece of the puzzle.

"That has to be where the immortals perform the ritual," Lyra said, her eyes fixed on the temple. "The place where they first bound themselves to the island."

Talon nodded, his expression grim. "And probably the place where they'll try to stop us."

"We have to go," Lyra said, her voice firm. "If we want to break the curse, we need to understand the full extent of the magic they used. That temple might hold the key."

Without another word, they began making their way down the steep path that led to the shoreline, the temple looming larger as they approached. The air grew colder the closer they got to the lake, and Lyra couldn't shake the feeling that they were being watched.

By the time they reached the edge of the water, the sense of unease had grown so thick it was almost suffocating. The lake's surface remained perfectly still, as if frozen in time, and the only sound was the soft crunch of their footsteps on the rocky shore.

"How do we cross?" Kael asked, frowning as he looked out at the expanse of water between them and the temple.

"There's a bridge," Sienna said, pointing to a narrow stone walkway that spanned the lake, connecting the shore to the temple. "But it doesn't look very sturdy."

"It's the only way," Lyra said. "We have to go."

They made their way onto the bridge, the stone beneath their feet slick with moisture from the mist that hovered over the lake. The further they walked, the more the oppressive stillness of the water seemed to close in around them, as though the lake itself was watching, waiting for them to make a misstep.

Halfway across, Lyra suddenly felt a strange sensation wash over her—a dizziness, a sense of disorientation that made her stumble. She reached out to steady herself against the railing, her heart pounding as the world around her seemed to tilt.

"Lyra?" Talon's voice was distant, muffled, as though he was speaking from far away.

Lyra blinked, trying to clear her vision, but the dizziness only grew worse. The lake, once still and calm, now seemed to ripple and shift, the reflections on its surface twisting into strange, distorted shapes. She could feel the pull of the island's magic, the ancient curse that bound the immortals, reaching out to her, tugging at the edges of her mind.

"Lyra, are you okay?" Sienna's voice cut through the haze, sharp and urgent.

"I'm fine," Lyra managed to say, though her voice felt weak, distant. "I just... I just need a moment."

But it wasn't just a moment. The dizziness was growing stronger, and with it, a flood of emotions that weren't her own. She could feel the weight of the immortals' curse pressing down on her, the centuries of isolation, the endless cycle of existence without purpose. It was overwhelming, suffocating, and it made her question everything.

Was this what they wanted? To live forever, trapped in a place that offered no escape, no peace? Was immortality really worth the price?

"Lyra!" Talon's hand was on her shoulder now, shaking her gently, trying to pull her back. "Stay with us. Don't let the island get into your head."

Lyra shook her head, trying to clear her thoughts. "I'm okay," she said, though the words felt hollow. "I just... I need to keep moving."

They pressed on, crossing the rest of the bridge in silence. Lyra could feel the weight of the curse hanging over her, like a dark cloud that refused to lift. The immortals had given up everything for the promise of eternal life, but what they had gained was an eternity of emptiness, trapped in a place where time stood still, where life had lost all meaning.

As they reached the temple's entrance, Lyra felt

a renewed sense of urgency. They couldn't let themselves fall into the same trap. They had to find a way to break the curse, to free themselves from the island's grip before it was too late.

The temple's interior was dark and cool, the air thick with the scent of ancient stone and dust. The walls were covered in more of the intricate carvings that seemed to pulse with a faint, golden light, and at the center of the room stood a large, circular altar, surrounded by candles that burned with an otherworldly glow.

"This is it," Lyra whispered, her eyes fixed on the altar. "This is where it all began."

As they approached the altar, Lyra noticed something strange—carved into the stone floor around the altar was a series of symbols, similar to the ones they had seen in the hidden chamber. But these symbols were different. They weren't just decorative—they were part of a spell, a binding ritual that had been performed centuries ago.

"This is how they did it," Lyra said, kneeling beside the altar to examine the symbols more closely. "This is how they bound themselves to the island."

"But why?" Sienna asked, her voice filled with frustration. "Why trap themselves here? If they wanted eternal life, why didn't they just leave and live forever somewhere else?"

"Because they couldn't," Lyra said, the realization hitting her like a wave. "The island's magic is tied to the cycle of life and death. They tried to escape death, but in doing so, they became bound to the island. The magic that gave them immortality also trapped them here. They can't leave because their immortality is tied to this place."

Kael's brow furrowed in confusion. "So they're not really immortal? They can't live forever without the island?"

"No," Lyra said. "Without the island's magic, they would die. They're not truly immortal—they're just trapped in a perpetual cycle of existence, unable to die but unable to live in any meaningful way."

Talon's face darkened, his voice filled with anger. "So they've been lying to us. They're not offering us immortality—they're offering us a prison."

Lyra nodded, her heart heavy with the weight of the truth. "Yes. And if we don't break the curse, we'll be trapped here just like them."

The realization was chilling. The immortals had once been like them—mortal, full of hopes and dreams. But their desire for eternal life had led them down a path of destruction, and now they were trapped in an existence that was worse than death.

Lyra stood, her gaze fixed on the altar. They had come here seeking immortality, but now she knew that immortality was not what they wanted. What they needed was freedom—freedom from the island, from the curse that bound them.

"We have to find a way to reverse the spell," Lyra said, her voice filled with determination. "If we can break the curse, we can free the immortals and ourselves."

"But how do we do that?" Sienna asked, her eyes filled with doubt. "This magic is ancient. We don't even know where to start."

Lyra took a deep breath, her mind racing as she tried to make sense of the symbols carved into the stone. "There has to be a way," she said. "The people who lived here before the immortals—they knew how to live in harmony with the cycle of life and death. If we can find a way to restore that balance, we can break the curse."

The group fell silent, the weight of their task pressing down on them. The island's magic was powerful, but it wasn't invincible. There had to be a way to undo the damage that had been done, to free themselves and the immortals from the prison of eternity.

"We'll find a way," Talon said, his voice filled with quiet determination. "We didn't come this far to give up now."

Lyra nodded, her heart swelling with resolve. They had come seeking answers, and now they had them. But the journey wasn't over yet. The island's curse was still hanging over them, and they would have to face it head-on if they wanted to survive.

As they left the temple and made their way back toward the forest, Lyra felt a renewed sense of purpose. The island's secrets had been revealed, and now it was up to them to decide what to do with that knowledge.

They weren't just fighting for their lives—they were fighting for their freedom. And they wouldn't stop until the curse of immortality was broken.

End of Chapter 10.

# Chapter 11: The Trial of Souls

The forest seemed to breathe around them, the air thick with the weight of unseen forces. Lyra could feel it in her bones—an ancient energy, raw and pulsing, pulling them toward something inevitable. It was as though the island itself was guiding them to their final test, the ultimate trial that would decide their fate.

The Trial of Souls.

They had heard whispers of it from the immortals, spoken in hushed tones, as if even uttering the name was dangerous. The Trial was the only way to leave the island or claim the immortality that had trapped so many before them. It was the final test—the one that would reveal their true selves.

As they walked through the dense, shadowed woods, Lyra's mind churned with thoughts of what lay ahead. The knowledge they had uncovered weighed heavily on her, as did the truth about the immortals and the curse that bound them to this place. But now, as they neared the heart of the island, the questions that haunted her were no longer about the island or its secrets—they were about herself.

What did she truly want? What was she willing to sacrifice for freedom, for life? Did she even want immortality anymore, knowing the price it exacted?

The silence between the group was heavy, each of them lost in their own thoughts as they approached the clearing where the trial would take place. Lyra could feel the tension in the air, the unspoken fears that swirled around them like mist. They had come so far, faced so many dangers, and now they were about to confront the most difficult challenge yet—themselves.

The clearing appeared suddenly, the trees parting to reveal a wide, circular space bathed in an eerie, silvery light. At the center of the clearing stood a massive stone altar, its surface covered in intricate carvings that glowed faintly in the dim light. Surrounding the altar were five stone pillars, each one taller than the last, forming a ring around the center of the clearing.

As they stepped into the clearing, the air grew cold, and Lyra felt a chill run down her spine. The Trial of Souls was not something that could be fought with swords or clever words—it was a test of the soul, a test that would strip away the lies they told themselves and reveal the truth of who they were.

"This is it," Sienna said, her voice barely above a whisper as she looked around the clearing. "The Trial."

Lyra nodded, her heart pounding in her chest. "We're ready."

But even as she said the words, she wasn't sure if they were true. Were any of them truly ready to face what was to come?

Galen, who had been quiet for most of the journey, stepped forward, his gaze fixed on the stone altar. "What do we do?"

Before anyone could answer, the ground beneath their feet trembled, and the air around them shimmered. The stone pillars surrounding the altar began to glow, each one pulsing with a different color—red, blue, green, yellow, and white. The light from the pillars grew brighter and brighter until it bathed the entire clearing in an otherworldly glow.

A voice, deep and resonant, echoed through the clearing, though it came from nowhere and everywhere at once.

"Welcome, travelers. You have come seeking immortality or escape, but first, you must face the truth of your own souls. The Trial of Souls will test your virtues, your morals, and the desires of your hearts. Only those who face the trial with honesty and courage may pass."

Lyra's breath caught in her throat. The voice was ancient, filled with a power that made her feel small and insignificant. She could sense the weight of the island's magic all around her, pressing down on her like a physical force.

"The trial is individual," the voice continued. "Each of you will face your own soul, your own choices. There is no right or wrong—only truth. But beware: the truth can be more dangerous than any sword."

The ground beneath their feet trembled again, and Lyra felt a strange pulling sensation in her chest, as though something deep inside her was being drawn out, exposed to the light. Her vision blurred, and the world around her seemed to spin. The others faded from view, their figures dissolving into the mist that now filled the clearing.

And then, everything went still.

Lyra blinked, and the mist cleared, revealing a new landscape. She was no longer in the clearing with her companions. She stood in a vast, empty field, the sky above her a dull, featureless gray. There were no trees, no mountains, no landmarks—just an endless expanse of barren earth stretching out in all directions.

For a moment, Lyra wondered if this was part of the trial, if she had been transported to some other realm. But then she saw it—a figure, standing in the distance, barely visible against the horizon.

The figure was small, but as it approached, Lyra's heart began to race. There was something familiar about the way it moved, the way it carried itself. And then, as the figure drew closer, Lyra's breath caught in her throat.

It was her.

The figure was an exact reflection of Lyra—her face, her clothes, even the way she held herself. But there was something different about this version of herself, something unsettling. The other Lyra's eyes were cold, calculating, and as she approached, a cruel smile played at the corners of her lips.

"Who are you?" Lyra demanded, though she already knew the answer.

"I'm you," the other Lyra said, her voice a mirror of Lyra's own, though it was filled with a mocking edge. "I'm the part of you that you try to hide. The part of you that you pretend doesn't exist."

Lyra's heart pounded in her chest. "What do you mean?"

The other Lyra stepped closer, her smile widening. "You're afraid, aren't you? Afraid of what you want. Afraid of the choices you've made. You tell yourself that you're doing this for noble reasons—that you're seeking the truth, that you're trying to help others. But deep down, you know the truth, don't you?"

Lyra's hands clenched into fists. "I don't know what you're talking about."

"Oh, but you do," the other Lyra said, her voice soft, almost soothing. "You want power. You've always wanted power. You came here because you wanted immortality. You wanted to live forever, to escape the fate that everyone else has to face."

"That's not true," Lyra said, her voice shaking. "I came here because I wanted to find the truth. I wanted to understand the island and what it means."

The other Lyra laughed, a harsh, grating sound that made Lyra's skin crawl. "You're lying to yourself. You want power. You want to be like the immortals. You want to control your own destiny, to live forever without fear of death."

Lyra shook her head, backing away from the other Lyra. "No... that's not true. I don't want that."

"Then why did you come here?" the other Lyra demanded, her voice growing harsher. "Why did you risk everything, leave everything behind? Was it really just for the truth? Or was it because you wanted something more?"

Lyra's heart raced as the other Lyra's words sank in. She had told herself that she came to the island seeking answers, that she wanted to understand the mysteries of life and death. But deep down, was that really the whole truth? Had she been chasing something else—something darker, more selfish?

The other Lyra stepped closer, her eyes gleaming with a cruel light. "You want power. You want control. You came here because you're afraid of death, because you want to escape it. Just like the immortals."

Lyra's breath caught in her throat, her mind racing with the weight of the words. Was it true? Had she come to the island not for answers, but for power? Had she been lying to herself all along?

"I... I don't know," Lyra whispered, her voice barely audible.

The other Lyra smiled, a cold, cruel smile that sent a shiver down Lyra's spine. "Admit it. You're just like them. You want to live forever, to be free from the fear of death. That's why you're here."

Lyra's heart pounded in her chest, her mind spinning. She had always prided herself on seeking the truth, on being willing to face the hard questions. But now, standing face-to-face with the darkest part of herself, she realized that the truth was far more complicated than she had ever imagined.

For a long moment, she stood there, staring at the other Lyra, her mind a whirlwind of conflicting emotions. She had come to the island seeking answers, but now she wasn't sure if she could trust her own motivations.

"I don't want power," Lyra said, her voice shaking. "I don't want to be like the immortals. I just... I just want to understand."

The other Lyra's smile faltered, and for a moment, something flickered in her eyes—something vulnerable, something that mirrored Lyra's own fear.

"You don't want to be like them," the other Lyra said, her voice softer now. "But you're afraid, aren't you? Afraid of what you'll find. Afraid that you'll never be able to go back to who you were before."

Lyra's heart ached with the truth of those words. She was afraid—afraid that she had changed, that the island had changed her in ways she couldn't undo. Afraid that she would never be able to return to the life she had once known.

But as she stood there, staring into the eyes of her own reflection, Lyra realized something else—something that cut through the fear and the doubt.

"I am afraid," Lyra said, her voice steady now. "But that doesn't mean I want power. It doesn't mean I want to be like them. I came here because I wanted to understand. And maybe I've made mistakes, maybe I've lied to myself. But I'm not going to let that define me."

The other Lyra's expression softened, and for a moment, she looked almost sad. "You can't escape who you are."

Lyra shook her head. "I'm not trying to escape. I'm trying to face it."

The other Lyra was silent for a long moment, her eyes searching Lyra's face. And then, slowly, she began to fade, dissolving into the mist like a ghost, leaving Lyra standing alone in the empty field.

Lyra's heart raced, her mind reeling from the intensity of the encounter. But as the other Lyra disappeared, she felt a strange sense of clarity. She had faced the darkest part of herself, and though the truth had been painful, she had survived it.

The Trial of Souls wasn't about power or control—it was about understanding. Understanding who she was, what she wanted, and what she was willing to sacrifice for it.

As the mist cleared, Lyra found herself back in the clearing, the stone pillars glowing softly around her. Her companions stood nearby, each of them looking shaken but determined.

Talon stepped forward, his eyes meeting hers. "Did you...?"

Lyra nodded, her voice soft but steady. "Yes. I faced it."

Sienna, her face pale but resolute, stepped closer. "We all did."

Galen, who had been silent throughout the trial, finally spoke, his voice filled with quiet determination. "We all had to face something. And now we know."

Kael, his brow furrowed in thought, nodded. "It wasn't about whether we wanted immortality. It was about whether we understood ourselves."

Lyra's heart swelled with a sense of solidarity. They had all faced the trial, and though each of their experiences had been different, they had come through it together.

The voice of the island, deep and resonant, echoed through the clearing once more.

"You have faced the truth of your souls. The path forward is open to you, but the choice remains. You may claim immortality, or you may leave the island. Choose wisely, for this choice is final."

Lyra's breath caught in her throat. This was the moment they had been waiting for—the moment of choice. But now, after everything they had learned, the choice didn't seem as clear as it once had.

Immortality was no longer the promise of freedom it had seemed. It was a trap, a prison that would strip them of their humanity. But leaving the island meant returning to the mortal world, to a life of uncertainty, of death.

Lyra glanced at her companions, each of them waiting for her to speak, to make the decision that would shape their future.

"I don't want immortality," Lyra said, her voice steady. "Not like this. I don't want to live forever if it means losing who I am."

Talon nodded, his expression grim. "Neither do I."

Sienna, her eyes filled with determination, stepped forward. "We leave. Together."

Galen and Kael both nodded in agreement, their faces set with resolve.

The voice of the island echoed one final time.

"Very well. The choice has been made. You are free to leave. But remember—there is no returning to this place. Once you leave, you will be bound by the cycle of life and death once more."

Lyra's heart swelled with a mixture of relief and sadness. They had made their choice. They would leave the island, and though their lives would be uncertain, they would face whatever came together.

As the pillars around them began to fade, the clearing dissolved into mist, and Lyra felt the weight of the island's magic lift from her shoulders.

They were free.

End of Chapter 11.

# Chapter 12: The Revelation of the Oracle

The mist was thick around them as they ventured deeper into the island, its tendrils wrapping around their legs and swirling at their feet as if alive. The air had shifted—no longer oppressive but strangely still, as if the very island was holding its breath, waiting for the final act to unfold. Lyra led the way, her heart pounding in her chest as they moved toward the center of the island, toward the heart of its mysteries.

The revelation of the Trial of Souls had changed them all, not just in spirit but in their understanding of what they had come for. The desire for immortality, once so clear, had become more complicated, more fraught with the knowledge they had uncovered. The immortals were prisoners of their own desires, bound to the island by the very thing they had sought to escape—death. But now, a new question loomed before them: Was there a way to transcend that fate? A way to find peace, not in eternal life, but in the wisdom that lay beyond it?

They were seeking the Oracle.

The legends said that the Oracle was the final guardian of the island, a being of immense power who held the answers to all the questions that had plagued them since they set foot on this cursed paradise. It was said that the Oracle could reveal the truth of immortality, the ultimate price, and the way to achieve harmony with the forces that governed life and death.

Lyra wasn't sure what to expect when they found the Oracle. Would it be a person, a god-like figure, or something entirely beyond comprehension? The weight of the moment pressed down on her as they approached the clearing where the Oracle was said to reside.

The trees around them parted suddenly, and they found themselves standing before a massive stone structure, far older than the council chamber or the temple they had encountered earlier. This building was ancient, its stone weathered and worn by time, the carvings barely visible through the layers of moss and vines that clung to its surface. It was as though the island itself had tried to hide this place from view, to keep it buried in the depths of time.

"This must be it," Sienna said, her voice a quiet whisper as she stepped forward. "The Oracle."

Lyra nodded, her heart racing. The structure loomed before them like a forgotten relic, its entrance a dark, gaping maw that seemed to swallow the light. There was no door, only a deep archway that led into the shadowed interior of the building. The air was cooler here, a chill that crept into Lyra's bones as they approached.

"Are we ready?" Talon asked, his hand resting on the hilt of his sword, though it was clear that no weapon would be of use where they were headed.

Lyra glanced at her companions, each of them looking back at her with a mixture of determination and fear. They had come too far to turn back now, but the weight of what lay ahead was palpable.

"We're ready," Lyra said, her voice steady despite the nerves that twisted in her stomach.

With that, they stepped into the darkness.

The interior of the structure was vast, the ceiling disappearing into shadows high above them. The walls were lined with more of the intricate carvings they had seen throughout the island, but these were different—more complex, more detailed, as if they told a story that had long been forgotten. The air was thick with the scent of age and dust, and their footsteps echoed eerily in the silence.

At the center of the chamber stood a single figure.

Lyra's breath caught in her throat as she realized that this figure was not like the immortals they had encountered before. The Oracle was neither male nor female, neither young nor old. Its form shifted subtly, almost imperceptibly, as if it was both there and not there, a being of both light and shadow. It stood still, its presence commanding yet serene, its face shrouded in a faint glow that obscured its features.

The Oracle turned toward them, though it did not move, and Lyra felt a strange warmth wash over her, as though the very essence of the being was reaching out to her soul.

"You have come," the Oracle said, its voice soft but powerful, like the rustling of leaves in the wind. It was not a voice that belonged to any one person—it was the voice of the island itself, ancient and all-knowing.

Lyra stepped forward, her heart pounding in her chest. "We seek the truth," she said, her voice trembling slightly. "We seek to understand immortality and the price it demands."

The Oracle's gaze, though unseen, seemed to pierce through her, through all of them, as if it could see their very souls laid bare. "You seek immortality, yet you fear the cost. You seek to escape death, yet you cling to the life you know. Do you understand what it is you truly seek?"

Lyra hesitated, unsure of how to answer. She had thought she knew—thought that immortality was something to be desired, a way to escape the inevitability of death. But now, after everything they had learned, she wasn't sure anymore.

The Oracle seemed to sense her uncertainty, and its voice softened. "Immortality is not a state of being. It is a state of mind. To live forever is not to escape death, but to live in harmony with the world, free from the fear that binds you to mortality."

Lyra frowned, her brow furrowing. "But... what does that mean? How can we live forever without immortality?"

The Oracle stepped closer, its presence overwhelming yet strangely comforting. "To live without fear, without greed, without the need for control—that is true immortality. It is not about living forever in a physical sense. It is about transcending the limitations of the mind, of the soul. Those who seek eternal life through the body will find only emptiness. But those who seek peace within will find eternity in every moment."

Lyra's heart raced as the words sank in. This was not the answer she had expected, but it made sense in a way that nothing else had. The immortals had sought to escape death by preserving their bodies, but in doing so, they had lost their souls. They had become trapped in a cycle of existence without purpose, without meaning. But true immortality wasn't about living forever—it was about living fully, without fear, without the need to control the passage of time.

"What about the immortals?" Talon asked, his voice filled with confusion. "They've been trapped here for centuries. Is there no way to free them?"

The Oracle turned its gaze toward him, and for a moment, the air seemed to still. "The immortals have trapped themselves, bound by their own desire for power. They cannot be freed until they choose to release themselves from the prison of their own minds. They must come to understand what you have learned—that immortality is not found in the body, but in the mind."

Sienna stepped forward, her eyes narrowing. "But what if they don't? What if they never realize the truth?"

The Oracle's voice was calm, unyielding. "Then they will remain as they are, forever bound to the island, forever seeking what they cannot find. It is their choice, as it is yours."

Lyra felt a wave of sadness wash over her. The immortals had sought to escape death, but in doing so, they had condemned themselves to an eternity of emptiness. They were prisoners of their own desires, unable to see the truth that had been in front of them all along.

"And what about us?" Kael asked quietly, his voice filled with uncertainty. "What do we do now?"

The Oracle's gaze returned to Lyra, its presence filling the chamber with a sense of quiet power. "You have a choice. You may leave the island, return to the world you know, and live your lives as mortals. Or you may stay, embrace the wisdom of the island, and find peace within yourselves. The choice is yours, but know this—true immortality cannot be forced. It can only be accepted, understood."

Lyra's heart pounded in her chest. This was the moment they had been moving toward since they had first arrived on the island. The moment of choice.

The Oracle had revealed the truth—immortality was not what they had thought. It wasn't about living forever in a physical sense, but about living without fear, without the need for control. It was about finding peace within, about accepting the natural cycle of life and death.

Lyra glanced at her companions, each of them lost in their own thoughts, their own internal struggles. She could see the weight of the decision on their faces, the uncertainty that lingered in their eyes.

"What do we do?" Galen asked, his voice barely above a whisper.

Lyra took a deep breath, her mind racing. She had come to the island seeking immortality, but now she realized that what she had been seeking wasn't the ability to live forever—it was the ability to live fully, to find peace in the face of uncertainty, in the face of death.

"I don't want to live forever," Lyra said quietly, her voice steady. "Not like the immortals. But I do want to live without fear. I want to live in harmony with the world, with myself."

Talon nodded, his expression thoughtful. "Yeah. I think that's what we've been looking for all along."

Sienna crossed her arms, her gaze fixed on the Oracle. "So what? We just accept that we're mortal and move on?"

The Oracle's voice was soft, almost gentle. "To accept your mortality is not to give up—it is to embrace the fullness of life. To live in harmony with the world is to understand that death is not an end, but a part of the cycle. When you let go of the need to control, to escape, you will find peace."

Kael stepped forward, his brow furrowed. "But what if we're not ready? What if we can't find that peace?"

The Oracle's gaze rested on him, its presence warm and steady. "The path to peace is not easy, nor is it immediate. It is a journey, one that requires patience, self-reflection, and understanding. But it is a journey worth taking, for it is the only path to true freedom."

Lyra's heart swelled with a sense of clarity. The Oracle was right. This was not about immortality—it was about freedom. The freedom to live without fear, without the need for control. The freedom to accept life as it was, in all its beauty and uncertainty.

"We can't stay here," Lyra said, her voice firm. "We need to leave the island. We need to live our lives, not as immortals, but as people who understand the value of life, of every moment we're given."

Talon smiled faintly, his eyes filled with a quiet resolve. "I'm with you, Lyra."

Sienna nodded, her gaze softening. "Yeah. Let's get out of here."

Galen and Kael both nodded in agreement, their expressions thoughtful but resolute.

The Oracle watched them in silence for a long moment, its presence a calm, steady force in the chamber. "Very well," it said finally. "You have made your choice. The path forward is open to you."

The air around them seemed to shift, and Lyra felt a strange lightness in her chest, as though a great weight had been lifted from her shoulders. The Oracle's words had given her the clarity she had been searching for, the understanding that immortality was not about escaping death, but about living without fear.

As they turned to leave the chamber, the Oracle's voice echoed one final time.

"Remember this: The true measure of life is not in its length, but in its depth. Live with courage, with compassion, and with an open heart, and you will find the peace you seek."

Lyra smiled, her heart swelling with a sense of purpose. They had come to the island seeking immortality, but they had found something far greater—wisdom, peace, and the understanding that life was not about escaping death, but about embracing every moment they were given.

As they stepped out into the light of the island, the path before them clear, Lyra knew that their journey was far from over. But now, they faced the world not as seekers of immortality, but as people who understood the true meaning of life.

And that, she realized, was the greatest gift of all.

End of Chapter 12.

# Chapter 13: The Betrayal

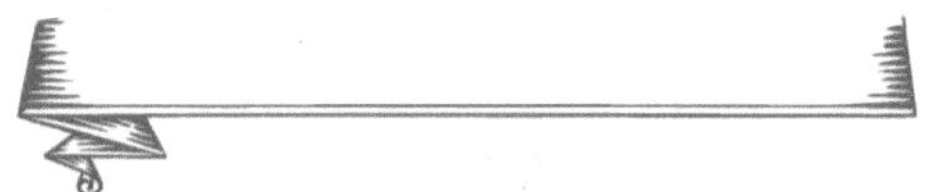

The sky above the island darkened as if in response to an unseen shift in the balance of its ancient magic. The warm, golden light that had bathed the island's forests, shores, and temples now felt cold and heavy, casting long shadows over the landscape. Lyra could feel the tension in the air as she and her companions made their way back from the Oracle's temple, each of them lost in thought after the profound revelations they had just experienced.

The Oracle's words had given them clarity—immortality was not the path they sought. Peace and harmony were what mattered, not the hollow promise of eternal life. Lyra could feel the weight of those truths pressing down on her with every step, but something else had been gnawing at her since they left the Oracle's presence. It was a feeling she couldn't quite name, something unsettling that flickered at the edges of her awareness.

The others were quiet as they walked, but there was a palpable tension among them, as if some invisible thread held them together, ready to snap at any moment.

As they approached the clearing where they had first entered the forest, the ground beneath their feet seemed to shift slightly, almost imperceptibly, but enough for Lyra to notice. She stopped, turning her gaze toward the others.

"Did you feel that?" she asked, her voice barely above a whisper.

Talon frowned, his hand resting instinctively on the hilt of his sword. "What was it?"

"I don't know," Lyra said, glancing around. The air felt thick with unease, and a faint tremor passed through the earth again. "Something's wrong."

Sienna stepped forward, her sharp eyes scanning the forest ahead. "Maybe the island's reacting to something. It's been acting strange since we met the Oracle."

Kael, who had been silent for most of the journey back, shifted uneasily. "We need to move. The Oracle said the path was open to us, but if we stay here too long—"

A loud crack split the air, cutting Kael off mid-sentence. The ground beneath them trembled violently, and Lyra stumbled as the earth seemed to heave beneath her feet.

"What's happening?" Galen shouted, his voice filled with panic as the ground shook again, more violently this time.

Before anyone could answer, the sound of running footsteps echoed through the trees, growing louder with each passing second. Lyra's heart raced as she turned toward the noise, her hand reaching instinctively for her dagger.

Out of the shadows, a figure emerged, moving quickly toward them. Lyra's breath caught in her throat as she recognized the face—Kael, but there was something different about him. His eyes, once filled with quiet determination, were now wild, frantic, and his movements were jerky, unsteady.

"Kael?" Lyra called out, confusion and concern twisting inside her. "What's going on?"

Kael stopped a few paces away from the group, his chest heaving as he struggled to catch his breath. There was a strange gleam in his eyes, something that sent a chill down Lyra's spine.

"They lied to us," Kael said, his voice shaking with a mixture of anger and desperation. "The Oracle... it wasn't telling us the whole truth. We don't have to leave the island. We can stay. We can take the power for ourselves."

Lyra's heart dropped, and a cold wave of dread washed over her. "What are you talking about?" she demanded, stepping forward. "We don't want immortality. We agreed—"

"No!" Kael shouted, cutting her off. "You don't understand. The Oracle was holding back. It doesn't want us to have the power. But I found something... something they were hiding."

Lyra's stomach twisted with unease as she glanced at the others. Talon's face was hard, his eyes narrowing as he took a step closer to Kael. Sienna's hand was on the hilt of her dagger, her expression unreadable, but Lyra could see the tension in her posture.

"What did you find, Kael?" Talon asked, his voice low and dangerous.

Kael's eyes gleamed with a manic intensity. "There's another way. A way to control the island, to claim its power for ourselves. The immortals— they were once like us, but they didn't understand the full extent of what the island could do. But we can. We can take the power, and we'll never have to leave. We can live forever, not like the immortals, trapped here, but as gods."

Lyra's blood ran cold. Kael had always been quiet, thoughtful, but there had been a growing restlessness in him ever since they had encountered the Oracle. Now, that restlessness had turned to something far more dangerous.

"This is madness," Lyra said, her voice trembling with disbelief. "We don't need that kind of power. The Oracle told us—"

"The Oracle was lying!" Kael snapped, his face contorting with anger. "It didn't want us to know the truth. It wanted to keep us weak, just like the immortals. But I won't be weak. I won't let this power slip away."

Lyra's heart raced as Kael's words sank in. She could see it now—the ambition, the desperation that had been festering inside him since they had arrived on the island. He had wanted immortality all along, but now it was clear that his desire for power had consumed him entirely.

"Kael, listen to me," Lyra said, trying to keep her voice calm despite the fear rising inside her. "This isn't the way. We came here to understand, not to take control. The island's magic—"

"Is ours for the taking!" Kael shouted, his voice cracking with emotion. "Don't you see? We don't have to leave. We can stay, and we'll never have to fear death again."

Talon stepped forward, his expression hard as stone. "This isn't about fear, Kael. This is about understanding what's right. You're being blinded by ambition."

Kael's face twisted with rage, and he drew his sword, the blade gleaming in the dim light. "You don't get to decide what's right! I've made my choice, and I'm not leaving this island without the power."

Lyra's heart pounded in her chest as she realized what was happening. Kael wasn't going to listen. He had made up his mind, and now he was willing to betray them all to seize the power he craved.

"Don't do this, Kael," Lyra said, her voice trembling. "You don't know what you're risking. The island—"

"I know exactly what I'm risking," Kael said, his voice cold and sharp. "And I'm willing to pay the price."

Before anyone could react, Kael turned and sprinted toward the center of the clearing, where a faint glow was beginning to emanate from the ground. Lyra's heart lurched as she realized what he was doing.

"He's going for the altar!" Sienna shouted, drawing her dagger and racing after him.

Talon and Galen followed close behind, their weapons drawn, but Kael was already too far ahead, moving with a speed and desperation that none of them could match.

Lyra's breath caught in her throat as she watched Kael reach the altar—a small, stone structure that had been hidden beneath the forest floor, its surface now glowing with an intense, otherworldly light. Kael reached out, his hand trembling as he touched the stone.

And then, everything went wrong.

The ground beneath them shook violently, a deafening roar filling the air as the earth cracked open. The light from the altar flared, blindingly bright, and the island itself seemed to scream in protest. Lyra stumbled, falling to her knees as the force of the tremor knocked her off balance.

"No!" she screamed, her voice lost in the chaos.

The air around them rippled with energy, a dark, swirling force that seemed to pulse with malevolence. The trees bent and swayed violently, their branches snapping and crashing to the ground as the island itself began to break apart.

Kael stood frozen by the altar, his hand still on the stone, his face twisted with a mixture of triumph and terror. The light from the altar enveloped him, but it was no longer the soft, golden glow of the island's magic—it was something darker, something corrupted.

The immortals appeared then, materializing out of the shadows, their faces twisted with rage and fear. The calm, serene expressions they had worn before were gone, replaced by something primal and furious. They moved toward the group with a speed that defied belief, their eyes glowing with an unnatural light.

"You have disrupted the balance!" one of the immortals shouted, their voice filled with anger. "You have broken the peace of the island!"

Kael turned to face them, his eyes wild with power. "I don't care about your balance! The power is mine now!"

The immortals surged forward, their movements fluid and unnatural as they descended upon the group. Sienna was the first to react, her dagger flashing in the dim light as she slashed at one of the immortals, but it was like striking air—the immortal moved too fast, too gracefully, dodging her attack with ease.

"Lyra, we need to get out of here!" Talon shouted, his sword drawn as he fended off another of the immortals.

But Lyra couldn't move. She was frozen in place, watching in horror as the island around them began to crumble. The trees were falling, the ground splitting open, and the

sky itself seemed to ripple and tear apart. The island was dying, its magic unraveling before their eyes.

"Kael, stop!" Lyra screamed, her voice filled with desperation. "You're destroying everything!"

But Kael wasn't listening. He stood by the altar, his body bathed in the dark light that pulsed from the stone, his face twisted with a manic grin. The power he had sought was now his, but it was tearing the island apart.

The immortals attacked with fury, their bodies moving in a blur as they struck at the group with inhuman speed and strength. Galen was thrown to the ground, blood pouring from a deep gash in his side, while Sienna fought desperately to hold them off, her movements swift but growing increasingly frantic.

"We have to leave!" Talon shouted again, grabbing Lyra's arm and pulling her to her feet. "Now!"

Lyra's mind raced as she stumbled away from the altar, her heart pounding in her chest. She could see the immortals closing in, their eyes filled with fury, their bodies moving with a terrifying grace. Kael had broken the balance, and now the island was turning against them.

As they fled, the ground beneath them continued to shake violently, cracks spreading across the earth like veins of some dark, terrible force. The island was collapsing, its magic tearing itself apart in response to Kael's betrayal.

Lyra glanced back over her shoulder, her breath catching in her throat as she saw Kael standing by the altar, his face lit with a dark, twisted joy. The power he had craved was now his, but it had come at a terrible price.

The island was dying, and they had to escape before it took them all with it.

But as they ran, Lyra couldn't shake the feeling that the worst was yet to come.

End of Chapter 13.

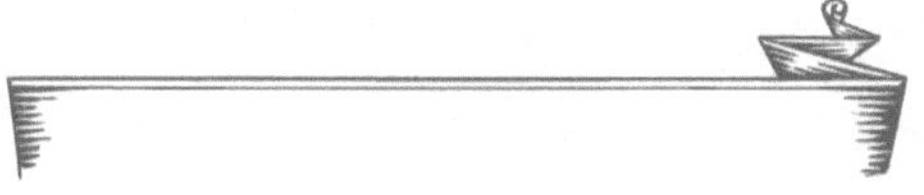

# Chapter 14: The Escape

The ground beneath Lyra's feet bucked violently, and the roar of the island tearing itself apart drowned out everything. She stumbled, barely catching herself as the earth cracked open, sending tremors through the once lush and serene forest. The air, which had once been filled with the sweet scent of flowers, was now thick with dust and the stench of something ancient and decaying. The island was crumbling, and they had to get out—fast.

"Lyra! Move!" Talon's voice cut through the chaos, his hand gripping her arm as he pulled her forward.

Her mind raced, still reeling from Kael's betrayal. His manic face flashed in her mind, his thirst for power so overwhelming that he had shattered the fragile balance of the island. Now, the immortals—once serene and seemingly invincible—were maddened, their rage palpable as they hunted them through the collapsing forest. But it wasn't just the immortals they had to worry about; the very island itself was turning against them.

"Where's Sienna?" Lyra gasped, scanning the chaotic landscape for their companion.

"She's ahead," Talon said, his voice tight with urgency. "Galen's with her. We need to keep moving or we'll never make it out!"

Lyra glanced behind them, her heart sinking as she saw the immortals closing in. Their once graceful, ageless forms now moved with a frantic speed, their faces twisted in rage and madness. The calm, ethereal beings they had first met were gone—replaced by something darker, something desperate.

"They're coming!" Lyra cried, her grip tightening on her dagger as she and Talon sprinted forward, dodging falling trees and jagged cracks in the earth.

Ahead, the landscape was shifting, the once familiar paths now twisted and distorted as if the island itself was trying to trap them. The ground heaved and splintered, sending chunks of rock and debris crashing down around them. Every step felt like a race against time, against the island's final death throes.

Lyra's heart pounded as they rounded a bend and saw Sienna and Galen up ahead, both of them struggling to navigate the treacherous terrain. Sienna's face was pale but determined, and Galen, though bloodied from the earlier fight with the immortals, was pushing forward with grim resolve.

"We need to head toward the coast!" Sienna shouted over the din, her voice strained but clear. "If we can reach the shore, we might be able to find a way off this island!"

Lyra nodded, the weight of the Oracle's words echoing in her mind. The Oracle had said the path forward was open to them, but that path was now crumbling. Still, there had to be a way—some way to navigate through the chaos and find safety.

The immortals' rage-filled cries echoed through the trees, growing louder as they drew closer. They were relentless, their movements inhumanly fast as they pursued the group through the collapsing island. Lyra could feel the weight of their presence, their anger, their desperation to reclaim what had been stolen from them.

"Lyra!" Galen's voice pulled her out of her thoughts, and she looked up just in time to see him pointing toward a narrow gap in the trees ahead. "That way!"

Without hesitation, they veered toward the gap, the ground trembling beneath them as they ran. The forest around them was falling apart, trees snapping like twigs and the earth cracking open in jagged, yawning chasms that seemed to swallow everything in their path.

As they ran, Lyra's mind raced. The Oracle had revealed the truth about the island, about immortality, and now she had to use that knowledge to save them. She had learned that the island's power wasn't something that could be taken or controlled—it was something that had to be understood, respected. The immortals, in their greed, had lost that understanding long ago, and now they were paying the price.

But how could she use that knowledge to save her friends?

"We're almost there!" Talon shouted, his voice breathless as they neared the edge of the forest.

Lyra's eyes widened as the trees parted, revealing the vast expanse of the ocean stretching out before them. The cliffs dropped sharply into the water, and below, the sea churned violently, as if the island's destruction had stirred the very waters around it.

"We need to find a way down!" Sienna yelled, her gaze darting around the rocky terrain. "We can't stay up here—this whole place is going to collapse!"

Lyra scanned the cliffs, her heart sinking as she realized just how steep and treacherous the descent would be. There was no easy path, no clear way to reach the shore. But they had no choice—they had to make it down before the island tore itself apart completely.

"There!" Galen pointed toward a narrow, crumbling path that wound its way down the side of the cliffs.

It wasn't much, but it was their only option.

Without wasting another moment, they sprinted toward the path, the ground shaking beneath them with each step. Behind them, the immortals' cries grew louder, closer. They were relentless, their fury driving them forward even as the island fell apart around them.

As they reached the edge of the cliffs, Lyra glanced back over her shoulder, her heart pounding. The immortals were closing in, their twisted forms moving with a speed and grace that defied the chaos around them. Their faces were contorted with rage, their eyes burning with the madness that had consumed them.

"Go!" Talon shouted, shoving Lyra forward. "We'll hold them off as long as we can!"

Lyra hesitated for a moment, her heart clenching at the thought of leaving them behind. But she knew they had no choice. If they didn't make it down to the shore, none of them would survive.

"Be careful!" she shouted, before turning and racing down the narrow path with Sienna and Galen.

The descent was treacherous, the path barely wide enough to support their weight as they made their way down the cliffs. The rocks crumbled beneath their feet, sending loose stones tumbling into the churning sea below. Every step felt like a gamble, but they had no other option.

Behind them, Lyra could hear the sounds of battle—Talon's shouts, the clash of metal, the inhuman cries of the immortals. She wanted to look back, to see if they were holding their own, but she forced herself to keep moving. They had to trust each other.

The path wound steeply down the cliffs, and Lyra's muscles burned with the effort of keeping her balance. The sea below roared and foamed, its waves crashing violently against the rocks, as if the very ocean was trying to swallow them whole.

"We're almost there!" Sienna gasped, her breath coming in ragged bursts as they neared the bottom.

Lyra's legs felt like they were on fire, but she pushed forward, her gaze fixed on the rocky shore just ahead. They were so close—if they could just reach the shore, they might have a chance.

But as they rounded the final bend in the path, Lyra's heart sank.

The shore was littered with debris—jagged rocks, fallen trees, and the remnants of ships that had been destroyed in the chaos of the island's collapse. The waves crashed against the rocks with a ferocity that made it clear escaping by sea would be nearly impossible.

"How are we supposed to get off this island?" Galen asked, his voice filled with desperation as he looked out at the tumultuous waters.

Lyra's mind raced, her thoughts flashing back to the Oracle's words. There had to be a way. The Oracle had said the path forward was open to them, that they could leave if they chose. But now, standing on the edge of the island with the sea raging around them, that path seemed anything but clear.

"Wait," Lyra said, her heart pounding as a thought struck her. "The island's power—it's connected to the balance of life and death, right? The Oracle said that immortality isn't about living forever, but about harmony."

"What are you saying?" Sienna asked, her brow furrowing in confusion.

Lyra took a deep breath, the pieces of the puzzle falling into place. "The island's collapsing because Kael disrupted that balance. But maybe... maybe we can restore it."

"How?" Galen asked, his voice filled with doubt.

Lyra's mind raced as she thought back to the Oracle's teachings. "We need to find a way to calm the island, to restore the balance it once had. The immortals were trying to control it, but we need to work with it. If we can do that, maybe the island will let us leave."

Sienna nodded, her gaze steady. "It's worth a shot. What do we need to do?"

Lyra glanced at the raging sea, her mind working frantically. "The island's magic is connected to the elements—the earth, the water, the air. If we can find a way to channel that energy, to calm it, we might be able to stabilize the island long enough to escape."

"But how do we do that?" Galen asked, his voice filled with uncertainty.

Lyra's eyes fell on a large, jagged rock formation jutting out of the cliffs nearby. "We'll need to create a focal point for the island's energy. If we can harness the magic that's still left, we might be able to redirect it and restore the balance."

Sienna and Galen exchanged a quick glance before nodding in agreement. "Let's do it," Sienna said, her voice filled with determination.

Together, they scrambled across the rocky shore toward the formation, their hearts pounding as the ground trembled beneath their feet. The island was still collapsing, but Lyra could feel a faint glimmer of hope—if they could just restore the balance, they might have a chance.

As they reached the formation, Lyra knelt beside the base of the rocks, her hands trembling as she began to focus her thoughts on the island's magic. She could feel the energy swirling around her, chaotic and raw, but beneath the surface, there was a deeper current—something ancient, something powerful.

"The Oracle said we had to find peace," Lyra murmured, her voice barely audible as she concentrated. "We have to let go of control, let go of our fear, and work with the island's magic."

Sienna knelt beside her, placing her hand on the rocks as well, while Galen stood watch, his eyes scanning the cliffs for any sign of the immortals.

Lyra closed her eyes, her breathing steady as she reached out with her mind, connecting with the island's energy. She could feel the chaos, the destruction that had been unleashed by Kael's betrayal, but she could also feel the island's desire for balance, for harmony.

"Focus," Lyra whispered, her voice filled with quiet determination. "We can do this."

The ground trembled beneath them, but Lyra remained still, her mind locked on the task at hand. Slowly, she began to feel the energy shift, the chaotic currents calming as she channeled the island's power through the rocks.

Sienna gasped as a faint glow began to emanate from the formation, a soft, golden light that pulsed with life. The air around them seemed to still, the wind dying down as the island's energy began to stabilize.

"It's working," Sienna whispered, her voice filled with awe.

But just as Lyra felt a glimmer of hope, a deafening roar echoed through the cliffs.

The immortals had found them.

Lyra's heart raced as she opened her eyes, her gaze locking onto the figures racing down the cliffs toward them. The immortals were relentless, their twisted forms moving with terrifying speed as they closed in on the group.

"Sienna, Galen!" Lyra shouted, her voice filled with urgency. "We need to hold them off until the island's magic is stable!"

Talon appeared from the shadows, his face bloodied but determined. "I'll help hold them back," he growled, drawing his sword as the immortals drew closer.

Sienna and Galen stood beside him, their weapons ready as the immortals descended upon them.

Lyra remained focused on the rocks, her hands trembling as she channeled the island's energy. The glow from the formation grew brighter, the air around them thick with magic as the island's balance slowly began to restore itself.

But the immortals were close, their eyes burning with fury as they closed in on the group.

"Hold them off!" Lyra shouted, her voice shaking with effort. "Just a little longer!"

Talon swung his sword, clashing with one of the immortals, while Sienna and Galen fought beside him, their movements swift and precise. The immortals were fast—too fast—but Lyra knew they couldn't give up. They had to hold out until the island's magic was restored.

As the battle raged around her, Lyra focused all her energy on the rocks, the light from the formation growing brighter and brighter until it was blinding. She could feel the island's magic stabilizing, the chaos beginning to subside as the balance was restored.

"Lyra!" Talon shouted, his voice filled with desperation. "Now!"

With a final surge of effort, Lyra channeled the island's magic into the formation, the golden light exploding outward in a wave of energy that swept across the shore.

The immortals screamed as the light engulfed them, their forms dissolving into mist as the island's balance was restored.

The ground beneath them stilled, the chaos of the collapsing island fading as the magic stabilized.

Lyra collapsed to the ground, her breath ragged as the glow from the rocks slowly faded. The island had been saved—for now.

"We did it," Sienna whispered, her voice filled with disbelief.

Lyra nodded weakly, her body trembling with exhaustion. They had survived. The island's magic had been restored, and the immortals were no longer a threat.

But as they looked out at the still, churning sea, Lyra knew their journey was far from over.

They still had to escape.

End of Chapter 14.

# Chapter 15: The Return and the Legacy

The waves crashed gently against the shore as Lyra stood on the deck of the small ship, her eyes fixed on the horizon where the island had disappeared into the distance. The sea was calm now, the chaos and fury of the island's collapse a fading memory, but the weight of everything they had experienced still hung heavy in the air. The salty breeze tugged at her hair, and for the first time in what felt like an eternity, Lyra allowed herself to breathe deeply, the tension in her body slowly easing.

They had survived.

Lyra glanced over at her remaining companions—Talon, Sienna, and Galen—each of them lost in their own thoughts as the ship sailed steadily back toward their world. The toll of their journey was etched into their faces, the scars of both physical and emotional wounds evident in their tired eyes. They had been through hell together, faced trials that had tested their strength, their resolve, and their very souls. But now, as they sailed away from the Island of the Immortals, they knew they had left something far more important behind.

Immortality wasn't about living forever.

It was about living a life full of purpose and meaning.

Lyra wrapped her arms around herself, staring out at the endless expanse of water. The Oracle's words echoed in her mind, as clear now as they had been when they had first left the island. True immortality wasn't a gift to be claimed or a curse to be avoided—it was a state of being, a way of living. It wasn't about the number of years one lived but about how one chose to live those years, the impact one left on the world and the people in it.

She had learned that lesson the hard way. They all had.

"How are you holding up?" Talon's voice cut through her thoughts, and Lyra turned to see him standing beside her, his expression soft but weary.

"I'm... still trying to process everything," Lyra admitted, her voice quiet. "It feels like a dream. Or maybe a nightmare. I don't know."

Talon nodded, his gaze drifting out toward the sea. "Yeah, I get that. It's hard to wrap your head around everything we've been through. But we made it out. That's what matters."

Lyra sighed, her heart heavy with conflicting emotions. "I keep thinking about Kael," she said softly, her mind flashing back to their friend's betrayal. "I keep wondering if there was something we could have done differently. Something I could have said..."

Talon's expression darkened, and he shook his head. "Kael made his choice, Lyra. It wasn't your fault. He let his ambition consume him, and in the end, he paid the price."

Lyra bit her lip, the pain of Kael's loss still fresh in her mind. She had cared for him, trusted him, and his betrayal had shaken her to her core. But Talon was right—Kael had made his choice, and nothing she could have said or done would have changed the outcome.

"I know," she whispered, her voice barely audible. "But it's hard not to think about what might have been."

Talon placed a comforting hand on her shoulder, his touch warm and reassuring. "We can't change the past, Lyra. All we can do is learn from it."

Lyra nodded, grateful for his presence. Talon had been her rock throughout their journey, always steady, always strong. She didn't know how she would have made it through without him.

"How do we move forward from this?" she asked, her voice tinged with uncertainty. "How do we go back to the way things were?"

Talon gave her a sad smile. "We don't go back. Not really. The island changed us, Lyra. We'll never be the same as we were before. But maybe that's a good thing. Maybe we needed to be changed."

Lyra looked up at him, her eyes searching his face. "Do you believe that?"

Talon shrugged, his gaze returning to the horizon. "I don't know. But I do know that we're alive, and that's something. We've been given a second chance to live our lives, and that's more than most people get."

Lyra fell silent, contemplating his words. He was right. They had survived, and now they had the chance to do something meaningful with the lives they had been given. The island had taught them that life was fragile, that time was precious, and that it was what they did with that time that truly mattered.

"We have to make sure the island's story is told," Lyra said, her voice firm with newfound resolve. "People need to know what happened there, what we learned. The lessons of the island can't be forgotten."

Talon nodded, his eyes reflecting her determination. "You're right. But how do we do that?"

Lyra thought for a moment, the answer coming to her as clearly as if it had been there all along. "I'll tell the story," she said softly. "I'll make sure people know. Not just about the island, but about everything we went through, about what we learned. I'll share the truth."

"You'll be a storyteller," Talon said, his voice filled with admiration. "That suits you."

Lyra smiled, a warmth spreading through her chest. "Yeah, I think it does."

They stood in silence for a moment, the sea stretching endlessly before them. There was a sense of peace now, a sense of closure. The island was behind them, but its lessons would stay with them forever.

Weeks passed after their return to the mainland, and the world around them resumed its normal rhythm, but Lyra and her companions knew they had been forever changed by their journey. The bustling streets, the laughter of children, the familiar faces of the villagers—it all seemed distant, as if it belonged to another life. They had come back to a world that hadn't changed, but they were no longer the same people who had left.

Lyra spent her days in quiet reflection, her mind replaying the events of the island over and over. She could still hear the Oracle's voice in her dreams, still feel the weight of the immortals' madness, and still remember the moment Kael had made his fateful choice. But through it all, one truth remained clear: the legacy of the Island of the Immortals needed to be preserved.

One evening, as the sun dipped low in the sky and bathed the village in golden light, Lyra sat down with parchment and quill. She had made her decision. She would write the story of the island, not just as a record of their journey but as a lesson for future generations. The story wasn't about her, or even about the immortals—it was about the deeper truths they had uncovered along the way.

She began to write.

*Once, there was an island hidden from the world, a place of great beauty and great danger, where those who sought immortality could find what they desired—at a price. The island was a place where time stood still, and those who lived there were forever trapped in the cycle of life and death, unable to leave, unable to move forward. But for those who understood its secrets, the island offered something far greater than eternal life. It offered the wisdom of how to live.*

As she wrote, Lyra found herself recalling each step of their journey in vivid detail—the discovery of the prophecy, the perils they had faced, the lessons they had learned from the Oracle. The island had tested them in ways they could never have imagined, but it had also given them the greatest gift of all: the understanding that life was not about living forever, but about living fully.

The story unfolded on the parchment before her, each word carrying the weight of their experiences, each sentence imbued with the knowledge they had gained. Lyra wrote about the immortals, about the price they had paid for their greed, and about how they had become prisoners of their own desires. She wrote about the Oracle and the revelation that immortality was not a physical state, but a state of mind. And she wrote about Kael—his ambition, his betrayal, and the lesson his fall had taught them all.

Hours passed as Lyra poured her heart into the story, her hand moving steadily across the parchment. The room around her faded into the background, and all that remained was the tale she was telling. It was a story of courage, of loss, of redemption, and of the power of living a life with purpose.

By the time she finished, the sun had long since set, and the room was bathed in the soft glow of candlelight. Lyra set down her quill and leaned back in her chair, her heart filled with a sense of completion. The story was finished, but it was only the beginning. It was her legacy—her way of ensuring that the lessons of the island would never be forgotten.

The next day, she gathered her companions—Talon, Sienna, and Galen—and shared the story with them. They listened in silence, their expressions shifting from sorrow to understanding as she recounted the events of their journey. When she finished, there was a heavy stillness in the room, as if the weight of the story lingered in the air.

"Thank you," Talon said quietly, his voice filled with emotion. "You've captured it all. Everything we went through, everything we learned... It's all there."

Sienna nodded, her eyes misty with unshed tears. "The world needs to hear this story, Lyra. People need to understand what we discovered on that island."

Galen, who had been the quietest of the group since their return, finally spoke, his voice soft but firm. "We may not have found immortality, but we found something far more important. And now, thanks to you, others will know too."

Lyra smiled, her heart swelling with gratitude for her friends. They had been through so much together, and now they were bound by more than just their shared experience—they were bound by the truth they had uncovered.

Over the weeks that followed, Lyra's story spread beyond the village, carried by word of mouth and by travelers who passed through. People from neighboring towns came to hear the tale, drawn by the legend of the Island of the Immortals. Some came seeking answers, others seeking solace, but all who heard the story left with a deeper understanding of what it meant to live a meaningful life.

Lyra became known as a storyteller, but she knew that the story wasn't truly hers. It belonged to the island, to the immortals, to Kael, and to all those who had come before them seeking immortality. It was a story that needed to be told, not just as a warning but as a reminder that life was precious, that time was fleeting, and that true immortality came not from living forever, but from living with purpose.

Years passed, and the legend of the Island of the Immortals became part of the world's lore, passed down from generation to generation. Lyra continued to tell the story, each time adding new layers of meaning, each time ensuring that the lessons of the island would never be forgotten.

And as she grew older, Lyra found peace in the knowledge that while she would not live forever, her legacy—her story—would.

End of Chapter 15.

# Don't miss out!

Visit the website below and you can sign up to receive emails whenever Patrick William Lee publishes a new book. There's no charge and no obligation.

https://books2read.com/r/B-A-FLRYB-YQWYE

BOOKS 2 READ

Connecting independent readers to independent writers.

Did you love *The Island of the Immortals*? Then you should read *The Dark Queen's Curse*[1] by Patrick William Lee!

In a kingdom plagued by dark magic, young Elara embarks on a perilous journey to break the curse of the ruthless Dark Queen. Guided by a prophecy and aided by unlikely allies, she faces mythical creatures, betrayal, and the Queen's overwhelming power. As Elara gathers ancient relics to defeat the Queen, she must decide between embracing her destiny or succumbing to the temptation of dark power. This thrilling tale of adventure, sacrifice, and redemption sets the stage for a new era of magic. Will Elara save the kingdom or lose everything in the process?

---

1. https://books2read.com/u/3LB9ON

2. https://books2read.com/u/3LB9ON

# About the Author

Patrick William Lee is a renowned author celebrated for his enchanting tales of magic and wonder. Specializing in the genres of fairy tales, folk tales, legends, and mythology, Patrick weaves stories that transport readers to fantastical realms where the impossible becomes reality. With a deep love for folklore and a talent for crafting timeless narratives, his books captivate the imaginations of readers young and old. When he's not writing, Patrick enjoys exploring ancient forests, studying mythical creatures, and sharing his passion for storytelling with audiences around the world. His works continue to inspire and delight, leaving a lasting impact on the world of literature.